D1453693

SANTA CLAUS
CONQUERS
THE
MARTIANS

SANTA CLAUS

CONQUERS

THE MARTIANS

Lou Harry

Roadside Amusements
an imprint of Chamberlain Bros.
a member of Penguin Group (USA) Inc.
New York

ROADSIDE AMUSEMENTS

an imprint of

CHAMBERLAIN BROS.

Published by the Penguin Group

Penguin Group (USA) Inc., 375 Hudson Street, New York, New York 10014, USA

Penguin Group (Canada), 90 Eglinton Avenue East, Suite 700, Toronto, Ontario M4P 2Y3, Canada (a division of Pearson Penguin Canada Inc.)

Penguin Books Ltd, 80 Strand, London WC2R 0RL, England

Penguin Ireland, 25 St Stephen's Green, Dublin 2, Ireland (a division of Penguin Books Ltd)

Penguin Group (Australia), 250 Camberwell Road, Camberwell, Victoria 3124, Australia (a division of Pearson Australia Group Pty Ltd)

Penguin Books India Pvt Ltd, 11 Community Centre, Panchsheel Park, New Delhi–110 017, India

Penguin Group (NZ), Cnr Airborne and Rosedale Roads, Albany, Auckland 1310, New Zealand (a division of Pearson New Zealand Ltd)

Penguin Books (South Africa) (Pty) Ltd, 24 Sturdee Avenue, Rosebank, Johannesburg 2196, South Africa

Penguin Books Ltd, Registered Offices: 80 Strand, London WC2R 0RL, England

Library of Congress Cataloging-in-Publication Data

Harry, Lou, date.

  Santa Claus conquers the martians / by Lou Harry

    p.   cm.

  ISBN 1-59609-163-0

  1. Kidnapping—Fiction. 2. Santa Claus—Fiction. 3. Mars (Planet)— Fiction. I. Title.

PS3608.A78386S23   2005   2005042686

813',54—dc22

Printed in the United States of America

10 9 8 7 6 5 4 3 2 1

Book design by Jaime Putorti

While the author has made every effort to provide accurate telephone numbers and Internet addresses at the time of publication, neither the publisher nor the author assumes any responsibility for errors, or for changes that occur after publication. Further, the publisher does not have any control over and does not assume any responsibility for author or third-party websites or their content.

SANTA CLAUS

CLAUS

CONQUERS

THE

MARTIANS

From a story by Paul F. Jacobson

As directed by Nicholas Webster

And recounted by Girmar of Mars,

daughter of Kimar and Momar

Acknowledgments

The author of the novelization would like to acknowledge the author of the screenplay who, he is sure, would like to acknowledge the person who had the idea in the first place. The author would also like to acknowledge that the views about Martians, Earthlings, Elves, and Santa Claus do not necessarily reflect those of the novelizer, or of his agents or publishers. The author would further like to acknowledge that he is not sure if novelizer is really a word. But wouldn't it be a better universe if it were?

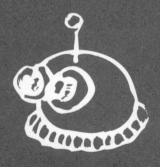

This book is dedicated to Michael Einbinder-Schatz,
Hans Kellner, Chris Richter, and Chris Starr,
fellow students of cinema.

Contents

Prologue

Testing. One. Two.

Testing.

Hooray for Santy Claus. One. Two.

Hooray for Santy Claus.

Is this working?

Hello.

Am I close enough to the primitive recording device?

Is . . .

Okay?

So you're ready.

Okay.

Name?

Okay.

My name is Girmar, daughter of Kimar and Momar.

No, I don't have a last name. Martians don't have last names. Have you not done any research before this interview?

Yes, I'm from Mars. Born and raised.

Yes, the Mars in the sky. Well, not in the sky, really. Past the sky. Way past. Why are you asking me. . . . ?

LOU HARRY

Oh, this is about the Santa Claus thing, isn't it?

No, I don't want a lawyer. Why should I need a lawyer? We don't have lawyers on Mars. One of the few benefits. You'd think with all the crater damage we get sometimes, that there'd be lawsuits. And with the people getting caught in our spiffy electronic doors. But no. No lawyers.

On Earth, the Tickle Ray would never have gotten on the market. Lawyers would have kept that from happening. What if someone should abuse the Tickle Ray? What if someone should trip and fall while self-administering the Tickle Ray?

In Mars . . . boom. Idea. Research and Development. Release. My father used to use the Tickle Ray on Dropo all the time. Dropo is . . .

Oh, okay. I'll slow down. Sorry.

You want to know about Santa, right? That's what this is all about. I figured as much. Once they find out who I am, everyone here in the hospital wants to know about what happened with Santa Claus. How Santa Claus conquered the Martians.

Well, "conquered" is a pretty serious exaggeration.

The truth?

Okay. I'll tell you the truth.

Because I was there.

1

In Which the Martian Children Watch Santa Claus on Their Video Machine

The video machine was a wondrous thing. Full of magic and life. In it, we saw men in hats riding creatures called horses. A crazed woman trying to operate a conveyor belt carrying confections. A uniformed man who kept threatening to send his wife to his planet's only moon. "Bang.

Zoom," we repeated. "Ricky, can I be in the show?" until our parents ordered us to stop. The adult Martians created the video machine as a way to study the cultures of other planets. We children saw it as a window to a world where people laughed without the help of a Tickle Ray.

LOU HARRY

The most wondrous thing we saw on the video machine, though, was not Lucy or Ralph or any member of the Cartwright clan. No, the most wondrous thing was a man in an oddly made red suit with white fur trim and a massive beard. He was the man Earthlings called Santa Claus. Beginning in the twelfth month of the Earth year—and sometimes sooner—his story would be told on the video machine in myriad ways.

I can't remember the first time I heard of him. I know it wasn't from my parents. It must have been my brother, Bomar. Because Bomar is ninety-seven years older than I, he got to watch a lot more video machine than I did. He was addicted to the video machine the way Sector 5 spousal units are addicted to the games of chance on Jupiter's third moon.

I remember before misting off to sleep, Bomar would tell me about Santa Claus and about toys and about the way this jolly man seemed to be everything that Martians were not. And his red suit was much more stylish than any of the green fashions we have here.

Why, on the so-called red planet, does everything look green? Just asking.

There was mystery around this man. How could one small polar factory produce enough toys for children around the Earth? How could he fit all these gifts in a sleigh? How could the wingless animals known as reindeer fly? Mystery upon mystery upon mystery with this white-bearded Earth man. Nobody here on Mars was as mysterious, except perhaps Chochem, who never had a holiday in his honor or a stop-motion animated special on the video machine. Santa had dozens.

The biggest mystery to me, though, was how Santa Claus seemed just a little different every time I saw him on the machine. Bigger cheeks one time. Rounder belly another. Longer beard. Shorter beard. Like he was a Venusian shape-shifter—only with an adaptivity level of three. Four at the most.

It was I who realized—and subsequently explained to Bomar—that there must be multiple secondary Santas, perhaps cloned from the original, who was housed at a frozen Earth point called the North Pole.

A good theory, I thought. But ultimately I was proven wrong.

The road toward that proof began when Bomar and I were, of course, watching the video machine.

An Earthling announcer on the screen stated that this broadcast was a special event. "A first in television history." And let me say now that I will never get used to the urgency of Earth newscasts. They seem to want the viewers to tense up at the very sound of a newsreader's voice. Martian newsreaders, on the other hand, traditionally recline on lounge chairs and sip fluorescent beverages during newscasts. It makes all the difference.

"At this moment, we are standing by with a television crew at Santa Claus's workshop," announced the announcer. "Andy Henderson, direct from the North Pole, braving the ninety-one-degrees-below-zero temperature, will bring a person-to-person interview with Santa Claus."

Yes, this truly was a special report. We would be seeing and hearing the real Santa Claus in just a matter of moments. The prospect was so exciting that my brother and I almost showed emotion.

"Hi, kids. This is Andy Henderson at the North Pole," the Earth reporter, presumably named Andy Henderson, said. "Wooo, it's cold up here. From this spot, there's only one direction you can go and that's south. Living up here is pretty rough. I don't see how Santa stands it. Since we've been here, we've eaten nothing but frozen food . . . at least, that's the way it is by the time we get it."

I think that was meant to be funny. With newsreaders, Martian or Earthling, you never can tell.

"Now," said the reporter, "let's take a look-see into Santa's workshop."

The Earth cameras then went into the workshop, a wondrous place filled with humans no taller than Bomar and I. A whole species whose life's work, it seems, was the creation of playthings for children.

Even at my young age, I wondered at their salary structure, what they did months out of the Earth year waiting for the holiday orders to come in, and if they ever found themselves short of food and had to kill off an underperforming reindeer. While these were all valid questions, I was confident that Henderson, being an Earth reporter, would fail to ask the really tough questions.

"Hello again," said Henderson. "Boys and girls, it's just weeks before Christmas and Santa and his helpers are working overtime to make sure there are enough toys for the kids all over the world. Santa is a pretty busy man, but I'm sure he'd like to say a few words to you kids."

And there, suddenly, was the great man himself, in all the standard accoutrements, including a pipe—which in a bizarre twist on the secondhand smoke problem, may have led to the diminutive stature of Santa's workforce, yet did not seem to impact him directly.

"Hello, Santa."

As Henderson approached, Santa himself was painting a toy. That's one of the things about Santa—involved in every step of production. It doesn't make for the most efficient workshop, but who can argue efficiency with a guy who makes all his deliveries in one night?

"Oh, hello, son," Santa said, pipe clinched between his teeth.

When he noticed the camera, he put down the toy he was working on.

"Oh, hello, boys and girls. Andy, you caught me at a very busy time."

"Well, do you think you'll be ready by Christmas Eve?"

"We've never disappointed the kids yet," said Santa.

"Earth kids, perhaps, but what about us Martians," I thought, but didn't say. After all, why upset Bomar? And why talk to a video machine?

"Tell me," said Henderson, preparing to scoop his rival Earth reporters. "There's a rumor that this year you're going to use a rocket sled. Is it true?"

"No, siree. We're going out the good old-fashioned way with my reindeer Prancer and Dancer and Thunder and Blitzen and Vixen and Nixon and . . . Nixon? Oh, where did I get . . . Oh, well. Consarnit, I get those names mixed up."

"But," he said, pointing to the camera, "the kids know their names."

Then another full-sized human pushed her way between the reporter and his subject. It was the woman who clearly was the pants-wearer in the Claus family.

"Santa, there you are," she said. "We have so much to do and you stand here dawdling, talking to this visitor."

"Mr. Henderson, this is Mrs. Claus."

I'd seen her represented before, a seemingly strong-willed woman, yet someone unable to hold on to a first name. Odd.

"Dear, we're on television," Santa tried to explain, in the way that I've noted male humans do when their spouses are demonstrating control in front of other humans.

"How do you do, Mr. Henderson?" she asked, but didn't wait for a reply. Instead, she turned to her husband and said, "Now, I want you to finish painting those hobbyhorses."

But then it registered.

"Television? Did you say we're on television? Oh, dear, why didn't you tell me?" she said, suddenly aware of the fact that her image was being beamed around the planet. Who knows what she would have done had she known that image was also traveling to every planet in the solar system (including Neptune, where, I've heard, reception is really poor).

"My hair's a mess," she continued. That messy coif didn't keep her from lighting up for the camera. "Hello, there."

But that was all she could say. She fiddled with her skirt, did a little dance of embarrassment, and rushed out of the range of the camera.

Santa laughed.

Santa laughs a lot.

Santa laughs a kind of hearty laugh I've only heard in movies on the Earth video broadcasts.

"Come along, Mr. Henderson, and I'll tell you about some of the new toys we're turning out," Santa offered. On Earth, it seemed, there were always new toys. What did they do with the old ones? I did not know, but Bomar told me stories about a place where toys go when they are no longer useful. He called it The Place of Good Will.

"How's it going, Winky?" Santa asked one of his hardworking elves.

"Everything is A-OK, Santa," said the elf.

"Good man," encouraged Santa. "Winky is in charge of our space department."

"Now, here is the latest toy rocket," he announced proudly, picking up a cylindrical object from Winky's worktable. "It runs on real rocket fuel."

What he showed was a device so primitive that any self-respecting Martian would be ashamed to present it at a lower-school science fair.

"Really?" said Henderson, but didn't wait for a response. He was too busy eyeing what looked like a green action figure amid the sawdust and wood chips. "I've been wondering what this strange little creature is."

"Oh, Winky made that," said Santa. "That's his idea of a Martian."

"A Martian," said Henderson. "Wow-wee-wow! I'd hate to meet a creature like that on a dark night." Henderson had been slipping the phrase "wow-wee-wow!" into every one of his interviews, hoping it would become a catchphrase that would sweep the nation. Using it with the Secretary General of the United Nations almost got him a demotion to weekend weather reporting.

"I wonder if there really are people on Mars?" Henderson pondered.

"Well," said Santa, not exactly contributing to the speculation. "Who knows?"

If Martians laughed, we would have laughed at that. But we don't, so we didn't. We just stared at the monitor, wishing we could tell Santa who we were and how much we wanted him to be here.

"If there are," said Henderson, "I hope they have someone like you up there, Santa, to bring joy and good cheer to all the Martian children."

"Oh, Mr. Henderson," said Santa modestly.

"Keep going, Winky, Christmas Eve is coming soon," encouraged Santa. "Now, Mr. Henderson, I want to show you some . . . "

And they were off, to another part of the workshop.

In the middle of the night—and I know I'm jumping ahead here—I heard my brother crying. I did. I heard him. Because the idea was implanted in his head that there could possibly be a Santa on Mars. And he knew that there wasn't. And there never would be.

2

In Which We Meet the Main Martian Players and Discover Their Dilemma

I should tell you about some of the key people in my world. You cannot understand what follows without knowing who they are.

There's Kimar. That's my father. A good man as far as Martians go. He is respected by just about everyone.

There's Lady Momar, my mother, who is everything a Martian mother and astrophysicist should be.

There's Voldar. He's the reason why I said that my father Kimar was respected by "just about everyone" and didn't say "everyone." *Now* it's fashionable to say that you knew Voldar was a bad, bad Martian. At the time, though, most Martians admired his strength, determination, and ability to squelch the Tandorian uprising. But I didn't like him even then. When he'd come to our pod for state dinners, he never washed his hands. And even then there was the persistent rumor that he had splat a man in Thimo, just to watch him fry.

And there's Dropo. How do I explain Dropo?

Well, I could tell you that my father could never find him. I could tell you that, when he did get found, he was usually sleeping. Which is why when Dropo was missing, my father would usually arm himself with the Tickle Ray when searching for him.

"Dropo. Dropo, you lazy good for nothing," Father said, on that particular occasion, as he searched—well, actually as he paced our spartan room. Every home on Mars in those days had a minimally furnished spartan room. We're not sure why.

"Where are you, Dropo? Dropo?"

His big mistake was that he was looking *across* the room rather than *down*.

Because Dropo was, of course, sleeping. This time under the table. In the past, we'd found him in the laundry chute, on the crevice of Cruax, and in the mindsweeper. It would have been a joke . . . if we knew what jokes were.

"Wake up. Wake up."

When words proved ineffective, Father took action, waving the Tickle Ray over Dropo's head.

The result was instantaneous. Before his eyes were even open, Dropo was a mess of giggles, struggling through them to say, "Turn that off."

Now, it might seem odd for such a humorless society to develop a weapon the likes of the Tickle Ray. I wish I had a logical response to that, but I don't, because the Martian culture is often contradictory and downright befuddling. For instance, we wear these helmets, which are enormously helpful in that they allow us to communicate with any of our fellow Martians just by thinking of that individual and mentally repeating our access number. That's fine. But most of these helmets also have a tube on the side that fulfills no function besides the decorative. Like I said, befuddling.

"Stand up. Stand up. Stand up. Stand up," ordered my father, turning off the Tickle Ray.

"I'm sorry, Chief Kimar, sir," said Dropo.

"Dropo, you are the laziest man on Mars," said Father. "Why are you sleeping during working hours?"

"I wasn't sleeping, Chief. It's just that I haven't been able to sleep these last few nights. I forgot how. So I was just practicing."

"Well, I suggest you practice doing your work," said Father who, to his credit, could have—and maybe should have—been more severe in his punishment. A little blast of the Tickle Ray wasn't going to change the ways of a Martian like Dropo. Not that there are a lot of Martians like Dropo.

The thing is, I think Father secretly enjoyed Dropo's antics. I think.

"Where's Lady Momar?" asked Father.

"Oh, she went to the food pill store to get some new food pills. The children haven't been eating well. No appetite at all."

"It's no wonder," said Father. "They sit in front of their video sets all day watching those ridiculous Earth programs. It confuses them. Where are they?"

"Oh," said Dropo, hating to tattle, "they're . . . watching Earth programs."

Father moved to the doorway, waved his hand, and it opened. That's another plus of the antenna helmet. No need for door handles.

In the next room, Bomar and I had our eyes glued to the screen, watching Andy Henderson and Santa Claus.

"Say, Santa, what have we here?" said Henderson, noting a bin of new toys.

"These are new dolls," said Santa. "Now, this little doll walks, talks, cries, and she even sings."

"Almost like a real live little girl."

"That she is, sir," said Santa. "That she is. All she needs is tender loving care."

No matter how many times we watched Santa, we were still confused by him.

"Bomar, what is a doll?" I asked.

"I don't know, Girmar," said my brother. "What is 'tender loving care'?"

"I don't know, either," I said.

"Bomar, Girmar, I told you not to watch these silly Earth programs. Now go to sleep," said Kimar.

Sometimes I like to call Kimar by his real name. Our names rhyme, kind of. That's either really cute or a real nightmare, depending on your age. As siblings, Bomar and I are not big fans of cute things. Mother used to have us wear identical leakage zappers when we were infanticals. How embarrassing is that? If we could turn red, we would have. Instead, we always looked kind of envious.

"Must we go to sleep now, Father? I want to see Santa Claus some more," I declared.

"I want to see more toys," said Bomar.

"No," said Father. "Go to sleep."

Father mentally shut off the video machine and we climbed into our disk beds as he dimmed the lights. With a shot from the mister over our heads, we were asleep. Until, as I mentioned before, I woke up to the sound of my brother crying.

Back in the spartan room, Dropo was adjusting some of the dials on the wall panel.

"Hello, Dropo, I see you are keeping busy," said Mother, who had returned from the store with our monthly supply of pills.

"I've been working really hard, Lady Momar," he said. "I've been vacuuming the roof." Thanks to Dropo, we had the cleanest roof in the zone. Which wasn't really that impressive when you consider that all of our dwelling units were underground.

"Good. Is the master here?" She sometimes called Father "the master." It was the closest thing anyone in the house besides Dropo made to a joke.

"He's in there," said Dropo, indicating our sleeping quarters. "And Kimar is very angry, too."

"Kimar," she said as he entered. "I brought some new food pills. I hope the children will eat these. We have hamburger. Buttered asparagus. Mashed potatoes. And a special treat for them—chocolate layer-cake pills."

"Momar, I'm worried about our children."

"So am I," she said. "They've hardly eaten a thing in three days."

"It goes deeper than that. They're behaving strangely. They appear to be troubled. They don't care to sleep. I had to use the sleep spray on them again."

(It had gotten to a point where Father was buying sleep spray by the case to use on us in the sleep mister.)

"I mentioned this to my council chiefs today and I learned that it's the same with children all around the planet in every district. Something is happening to the children of Mars," said Father, who should have seen this coming for years—at least ever since Bomar's Blintzva Nintzva party, when nobody would participate in the traditional throwing of the hair clippings.

"Kimar," said Mother, "as leader of the Martians, you must do something about it." She was prone to making statements that included bits of exposition.

"I know," he said, ever the weary leader. "But what?"

Of course, she already had an idea in mind.

"Why don't you go to the forest and see Chochem, the ancient one? He'll know what to do. He has never failed you."

To us, all adults were ancient ones. But this guy, well, this guy was seriously ancient. This guy was so old, he blitzplugged Mars dust. That's how old he was. This guy was so old, when he was born, the hologram of Lady Smeelee was only a pod print. I'm talking old.

"You speak wisely," declared Father. "I will go."

And with a touch of his belt buckle, which opened up his antenna line, Father summoned his trusted team.

"Attention, council chiefs. Please report."

"Lomas reporting," came a voice.

"Rigna reporting," came another.

"Hargo here."

There was one missing.

"Voldar?" said Father. "Voldar, please report."

After a moment, the voice that always caused Bomar and I to get plegpleg pimples up and down our arms came through.

"Voldar reporting."

"Gentlemen of the council, we will meet immediately in front of Chochem's Chair in Fronter Forest."

"What's wrong now, Kimar?" asked Voldar, as if he couldn't be bothered with such trivialities.

"I don't know, Voldar. But I mean to find out."

3

In Which Kimar and Crew Visit Chochem's Chair for Sage Advice

How to describe Chochem's Chair?

Imagine the inside of your nostril.

Now make it grosser.

Now add a little smoke. And cobwebs.

Now you're getting close.

This is where the council—Father's most trusted team—gathered.

"Where's Kimar?" asked Voldar indignantly.

"He should be here any moment," said Hargo, the scruffy bearded one. Bomar got in trouble once at

Academy for spreading a rumor that a family of zepoks lived in Hargo's beard. Twenty years later, the band Hargo's Beard had a series of hit recordings on three planets. Pretty good for a band where the lead singer was cyborg.

"What's this all about?" Voldar wanted to know.

"We'll find out when Kimar arrives," answered Hargo. "We are probably going to seek the advice of Chochem."

"What does Kimar think we are?" grumbled Voldar. "A kindergarten class? Can't we make our own decisions? Must we always come crawling to the doddering old man?"

"Chochem is eight hundred years old," said Rigna, who is rumored to have read the entire *Encyclopedia Mestamophades*. "You can't dismiss the wisdom of centuries."

"I can," declared Voldar, just as Father arrived from out of the mist.

"Gentlemen, thank you for coming," he said, as they all turned to face the mystical Chair of Chochem. This wasn't the first mystical Chair of Chochem. Actually, the original was in the Museum of the Ancients. But this one was believed to do just fine.

"Chochem, are you here?" asked Father. "Ancient

one of Mars, I call upon you, Chochem. It is I, Kimar, and the council chiefs. We need you, Chochem."

And in a flash of smoke he was there, carrying the famous wooden staff two feet taller than his head.

Imagine your Larry King, the Dalai Lama, Yoda, and the *Lord of the Rings* wizard guy all rolled into one and then kind of stretched out. That's him.

"You called me, Kimar?" he croaked.

"We need your advice, Chochem."

This, in hindsight, would seem to be stating the obvious. Chochem isn't the kind of figure you would just pop in on to say "hi." You'd have to have a very good reason, like needing parenting advice.

"Something is wrong with our children," Father said, suddenly sounding a little on the pretentious side. Which, I suppose, is a common reaction when one is suddenly in the presence of a spirit or sooth-sayer. "They eat not. They sleep not. Their only interest is watching meaningless Earth programs on the video."

"What time of year is it now?" asked Chochem, never one for meteorology or astrology, but always one to cut to the chase.

"It is the middle of Septober," answered Father.

"Oh, no. I mean on Earth. Ah, yes, it is early December on Earth, the time of the Christmas," said Chochem. "That explains it."

"What is a Christmas?" asked Father.

"It is an occasion of great joy and peace on the planet Earth," said the wise one. "And for children, it is also a time of anticipation as they await the arrival of Santa Claus and his gifts."

Apparently, Chochem had himself a video machine as well.

"Bah, what nonsense," muttered Voldar, not something you really should say to an ancient one.

"Ancient one," asked Father, "what does this have to do with our children?"

"We have no children on Mars," Chochem explained, with more than a touch of sadness in his voice. "They have children's bodies but with adult minds. They do not have childhoods."

Father knew exactly what Chochem meant.

"I've seen this coming for centuries," continued the ancient one. "They are born. Our electronic teaching machines are attached to their brains while they are in their cradles. Information is getting to their minds in a constant stream, and by the time they can walk they are adults. They've never played. They've never learned to have fun, and now, now they are rebelling."

The Martians stood there, knowing that Chochem not only was never wrong, but never uttered a word that didn't need to be said.

"What do you advise?" asked Father.

The word "advise" may not have been the right one here. For whatever Chochem advised, Father would surely follow. You want wisdom? You go to this guy. This guy sweats wisdom. And if you don't plan on following the path laid out by Chochem, why ask his advice in the first place?

"The children must be allowed to be children again," declared Chochem. "They must learn to play. They must learn what it means to have fun."

And as if the group hadn't jumped to this conclusion themselves, Chochem added, "We need a Santá Claus on Mars."

Then there was thunder. His body shook.

There was a puff of smoke.

And he was gone.

If one were in a contrary mood, one might ask why Chochem didn't give us this wisdom many, many years ago. But perhaps one shouldn't ask such questions to one so wise. And perhaps Chochem can only answer that which is asked.

"Santa Claus on Mars?" asked Lomas, the usually silent one.

"Where do we get a Santa Claus?" wondered Rigna.

"There's only one Santa Claus," said Father, trying to understand the path that had been laid before him by Chochem. "And he's on Earth."

Voldar laughed. "Well, I guess that takes care of

that. Didn't I tell you it was a foolish idea to seek advice from that old man?"

"This is a serious matter, Voldar," said Father, "and desperate problems require desperate deeds. Earth has had Santa Claus long enough. We will bring him to Mars."

"I'm against it," was Voldar's expected reply. I should add that Voldar is known in some circles as Voldar the Childless. (Yes, I know, it's not very nice. But neither is he.) "Our children are fine the way they are. I don't want any Santa Claus bringing them toys and games. They'll start playing and laughing and running underfoot. They'll become a nuisance. . . . "

See what I mean about creepy?

"I've made my decision," announced Father. "We leave for Earth tonight. Rigna, Lomas, prepare *Spaceship Number 1.*"

Now, *Spaceship Number 1* was the number one spaceship, hence its name. We never would have named it *Spaceship Number 1* if we didn't think it was the best . . . although I suppose we might have named it *Spaceship Number 1* if it was the best at the time we built it, but then we built another spaceship and we would have faced the dilemma of naming that one *Spaceship Number 1-Now* or *Spaceship Number 1-A*, or changing the name of the first best one to the *Spaceship Formerly Known as Spaceship Number 1*. So maybe it wasn't our best, but I'm not sure why our leader would rocket to Earth in a ship that wasn't our best.

I was a child then. I could not know everything . . . although, as Chochem said, we weren't really children.

By the way, about those electronic teaching machines that Chochem mentioned: They were not very healthy . . . but we didn't know that. Since they were hooked up to our brains we didn't actually have classes or classmates. Which means that we would always get caught passing mental notes to ourselves. And dodgeball games during recess were really, really dull.

4

In Which the Martians Travel to Earth and Engage in Operation: Santa Claus

Father, Voldar, Rigna, and Hargo sat at their stations on the bridge of *Spaceship Number 1*, concentrating on their tasks. Father had the best view through the view window into the deep recesses of space. Except when Hargo wore a big hat.

"Approaching projected Earth orbit," said Father. "Fire portside rockets number one and number two."

"Portside rockets number one and number two fired," reported Voldar.

"Entering Earth orbit," noted Father. And like the rest of the crew of this valiant ship, he experienced none of the dramatic effects so popular in Earth videos. There was no jolting from side to side. No spilling out of one's seat. No rolling about on the floor. Entering an orbit was like walking through a doorway from one room to another. All you heard was a little *pffffttt* sound, like a small herd of legaloaf passing gas. Only less stinky.

"All right, Voldar," said Father. "Now to find Santa Claus. Turn on your magnascope to third power."

He did. And the awesome visionary power of the magnascope was displayed.

"We're over a city of some kind," observed Father.

Voldar wasn't impressed. "So that's what the Earth people call a city, eh?" he said. "How primitive. Look at all those buildings *above*ground. Why, we could destroy that city with one blast of our Q-ray."

And, let me be clear about this, the ship was equipped with a fully armed Q-ray. It came standard in those days.

"We did not come here to destroy anyone," corrected Father. "Our only purpose is to bring Santa Claus back to Mars. Turn to fifth power. See if we can locate Santa Claus. He wears a red suit trimmed with white fur and he has a long, white beard."

"But there are millions of people down there,"

said Voldar. "It's like looking for a speck of space dust in a comet's tail."

But that speck of dust wasn't as elusive as Voldar thought.

"Wait a minute," he said, just moments after complaining of the impossible odds against finding their prey. "I see him. I see Santa Claus."

Through the tight circle of his magnascope screen, he saw, yes, a man in a red suit with white fur trim wearing a long, white beard.

"I see him, too," said Father, looking in a location hundreds of miles away.

"He's standing on a corner ringing a bell," said Voldar.

"No he's not," said Father. "He's standing near the entrance of a large building near a big, black kettle."

"He's standing on the corner, Kimar. He . . . Wait a minute. I see another one."

"Why, there are hundreds of them down there," said Father.

"Are we going to bring them all back with us to Mars?" asked Voldar.

"Just one," said Father, not quite grasping the whole Santa Claus concept. "And with so many, they won't miss one. Prepare for landing on next orbit."

While the crew of *Spaceship Number 1* was tracking Santas, the people of Earth were having their television programs interrupted for a news bulletin. As with most such interruptions, Earthlings immediately leaped into action and started calling their stations, complaining that episodes of *Bewitched*, *Voyage to the Bottom of the Sea*, *The Man from U.N.C.L.E.*, *Shindig*, *Gomer Pyle USMC*, and, ironically, *The Outer Limits* were being preempted. Interestingly, nobody called to complain about the preemption of the *Beverly Hillbillies*-ish series *The Baileys of Balboa*, starring Paul Ford, Clint Howard, Sterling Holloway, and Judy Carne.

"We interrupt this program for a special UFO bulletin," said the announcer. "An unidentified object has been spotted in orbit around Earth. The Soviet Union denies it has launched any new space satellites. Our radar stations are tracking the spaceship . . . or whatever it is. The U.S. Air Force has alerted all defense commands and retaliatory units. Stay tuned for further bulletins."

Their actions were noticed by the surprised crew of *Spaceship Number 1*.

"Sir," said Rigna. "Earth radar beams are bouncing off our ship." This they all knew should not happen when your radar shields are up.

"Well, it certainly took them long enough," said Voldar as Father ordered him to check on the shields.

But there was something wrong. The whole crew knew there was something wrong.

"Misfunctioning of radar shields," announced Voldar.

Rigna, the least experienced of the crew, feared the worst—that the ship's electrical system had shorted. If that should happen, the radar screen would be the first thing to go. Then a series of other malfunctions would follow, climaxing with the ship spinning wildly out of control and, upon contact with even the smallest particle of floating debris, exploding into a trillion pieces. Rigna had experienced that scenario at spaceship school during simulation finals, and had been ridiculed about it by his fellow students ever since. Sometimes they just call him on the helmet antenna, say "boom," and laugh.

But Father knew that the first step toward dealing with a crisis was determining the most likely problem, not the least likely.

"Rigna," he said. "Check the radar box."

And that's what he did.

The problem was not difficult to diagnose. This, Rigna found, was not a case of a malfunctioning electrical system or a misprogrammed cardameter. It was, in Rigna's words, "a slight case of Dropo," he said, pulling the troublesome Martian out of the radar box.

"Hi, Chief," said Dropo, as if casually running into his leader at the antigravity gym.

"What are you doing here, Dropo?" asked Father, as Rigna restarted the radar system.

"Well, Chief," said Dropo, "I went to the launching pad to say good-bye to you and I remembered, I'd never been to Earth. So I thought I'd . . . "

Father had heard enough. "I may leave you there in place of Santa Claus. Now, get below. I'll deal with you later."

As if genetically incapable of not making a mess of things, Dropo reached for some switches and started randomly pulling them.

"Dropo, get below quickly," barked Father.

"Yes, Chief. I'm sorry."

And in his own way, he was.

"Prepare to land," said Father, returning to the more important business at hand. "We'll set down in that field near the lake."

"Rocket silencer set," said Rigna, hiding his fear.

"Rotor rockets numbers one and two fired," Voldar said. Voldar loved firing rockets.

And with a minor, minor jolt, they were ready to land.

"All this trouble," scowled Voldar, "over a fat little man in a red suit."

⚭

On Earth, there was another interruption of television programming.

"Here's another UFO bulletin," said the announcer. "The Defense Department has just announced that the unidentified flying object has suddenly disappeared from our radar screens. They believe the object has either disintegrated in space or that it may be a spaceship from some other planet, which has the ability to nullify our radar beams. Because of the ominous situation, the president has ordered the strategic air command into action."

And into action they went. Sirens blared. Men ran to their planes and climbed into the cockpits. The Air Force was in the air in force. Nobody on Earth, it seemed, could look into the sky without seeing a proud flyer airborne, prepared to deal with the potentially aggressive force from beyond. In hindsight, it's pretty amazing that my own father wielded such power. My friend Fridar's father was only a dry cleaner.

But for all his power, Father wasn't always able to control everything in his, pardon the expression, orbit.

"Fire retro rockets numbers five and six," ordered Father. These weren't rockets of offense; they were landing rockets, necessary to ease the ship to its resting place on this blue-skied planet.

"Retro rockets numbers five and six fired," responded Voldar, when the proper button had been pushed and the really cool sounds had been made. I love the sound of retro rockets numbers five and six. For a while, I had my morning alarm programmed to make that sound.

"Lower landing legs," ordered Father.

Rigna pulled the appropriate levers.

"Landing legs lowered," said Rigna.

It is amazing how the blandest of conversations can result in the most miraculous actions. With those words, Martians had landed on Earth. Even though Martians have explored most of the solar system (you should see the nightlife on Uranus), it still amazes me that such journeys are possible. But, then again, I'm still fascinated by escalators. I mean, where do the stairs go?

"Attention, crew, this is Kimar. When we've landed, Rigna, Voldar, and I will leave the ship to investigate." Because, as we later learned from *Star Trek*, it's always best when the captain joins a ship's landing parties. "Hargo, Lomas, and Dropo will stay on board on constant alert for immediate blastoff."

And with that, they prepared for Operation: Santa Claus.

5

In Which We Meet the Earth Children Betty and Billy

Thehe story of the mysterious ship not only made a mess out of Earth's television schedule, it also dominated the radio waves.

Radio, in case you aren't familiar, is like Earth video, only with your eyes closed.

"The Defense Department believes that the object spotted on our radar screens might be nothing more than a meteor which broke up when it entered our atmosphere," spoke the radio newscaster.

"Professor Werner Von Green, our leading space

expert, is convinced that it was a Martian spaceship. Stay tuned for further bulletins."

A little girl turned off her radio, not really in the mood to await further bulletins. But that doesn't mean she wasn't curious about what she was hearing.

"Billy," she asked, "what does a Martian look like?"

She was talking to her brother, who was so fascinated by all things spacelike that he had brought the radio outside with them so as not to miss a bit of the news.

"I don't know," said the boy. "Nobody's ever seen one."

"I don't believe there are any Martians," said the girl.

"You don't, huh?" he said. "What would you do if a Martian walked right up behind you?"

"I'd scream," she answered, matter-of-factly.

And as if on cue, Father and his landing party walked up behind her.

And she saw.

And she screamed.

To hear my father describe it, I'm surprised they didn't hear it on Mars.

"Aw, stop, Betty, I'm trying to relax," said her

brother, in one of the most insensitive moments in the history of sibling relationships.

"I see a Martian," she managed to say.

"Boy, you and your imagination," he said dismissively. "Come on, let's go inside."

But then he turned. And he saw. And for the first time in his short life, he had no idea what to say. You could practically see the confidence draining from his face.

"Oh, who are you?" he managed to ask.

"We're from Mars," my father tried to explain. "Don't be afraid. We have children just like you on Mars."

The kids began to adapt to the situation. Earth children are good at that. Their curiosity seems to circumnavigate their fear.

"What are those funny things sticking out of your head?" asked Betty. If I had asked something that insensitive, my father would have removed my bytrillium privileges. But with the Earth kid, he was Mr. Nice.

"Those are our antennae," explained Father.

"Are you a television set?" she asked.

"Shh," Billy said, but Father just went with it and smiled.

"Stupid question," said Voldar. "Is this what you want to do to our children on Mars, turn them into nincompoops like these?"

"Hold your tongue, Voldar," said Father. "What's your name, little boy?"

"Billy, Billy Foster, sir. And this is my sister, Betty."

"Perhaps you can help us, Billy. We're looking for one of your Santa Clauses."

"There's only one Santa Claus," the boy insisted.

"We've seen many of them in your cities," said Rigna.

"Oh," said Billy, beginning to feel confident as he realized that he knew something the Martians didn't. "Those are his helpers. There's only one real Santa Claus and he's in his workshop up at the North Pole."

Then he realized that maybe he shouldn't give any information. What did they say in the spy movies are the only things you are supposed to say when you're captured by the enemy? He tried to remember. Name, rank, and social security number? Something like that. But surely if the Martians were capable of building a ship for interplanetary travel, they were capable of doing the minimal pre-mission research of finding out where Santa lived.

Or maybe not.

"That's what we came here to find out," said Father. "Let's go."

"Come on, you two," said Voldar, not wanting to leave any witnesses behind. He grabbed each of them by an arm.

"Let me go," said Betty.

"Where are you taking us?" asked Billy.

"Leave them alone, Voldar," said Father.

"What? And leave them here to inform the authorities?"

"He's right, Kimar," said Rigna. "We'd better take them along with us to the North Pole." Rigna could surprise you every once in a while by being the voice of reason. I expect that when my father reaches the mandatory retirement age in four hundred thirty-three years, Rigna will take over.

While Father agreed to the plan, the children—who had never been north of Welch Lake—weren't so sure. Not that they had any say in the matter.

6

In Which Betty and Billy Overhear the Martians' Plan

Here on Mars, we heard it on the video machine.

"This morning, two children disappeared mysteriously from the vicinity of Welch Lake. The police have found no clues, and it seems as though Billy and Betty Foster have simply vanished into thin air. This appears to be a day when everything is vanishing into thin air. Local police are continuing their search for the missing children. The armed forces are continuing their search for the mysterious object from space."

During the report, we saw footage of the crude earth airships in the air—including a shot that I believe was lifted from the movie *Dr. Strangelove*. We love early Stanley Kubrick flicks up here on Mars.

While I'm on the subject, let me tell you about five Earth movies that we really enjoy on Mars:

The War of the Worlds. In this classic 1950s adaptation of H. G. Wells's novel, we Martians kick Earth butt—until we catch a cold. Not to be confused with the Steven Spielberg version.

Red Planet. This is actually a fairly decent Val Kilmer science-fiction movie.

Mars Needs Women (1967). Okay, we didn't see it. But we love the title.

Eyes of Laura Mars. Not really about the planet Mars—and not really a good movie—but it's kind of fun to have this thriller on the list. It stars an actress named Faye Dunaway, and Martians always like names that kind of rhyme.

Ziggy Stardust and the Spiders from Mars concert film. Similar to *Eyes of Laura Mars*, only without Faye Dunaway and not really a thriller. Okay, so it's nothing like *Eyes of Laura Mars*. It's really a concert movie featuring a singer named David Bowie, but he's playing a singer named Ziggy Stardust. At least, that's what we think is going on. We're not really too up on the whole rock-and-roll thing because, as a species, it is impossible for us to keep a beat.

On the other hand, here are the four Earth movies about Mars that were given the Limp Antenna Award at the recent Let's Make Fun of Earth Bad Film Festival.

Red Planet Mars. In this one, it turns out that signals coming from Mars are actually messages from God. We know we're superior, but we're not *that* superior.

Mission to Mars. I have yet to meet a Martian that likes any Brian De Palma film besides *The Untouchables.* I have no explanation for this.

Robot Monster. The title creature looks—I swear—like a guy in a gorilla suit wearing a diving helmet.

Frankenstein Meets the Space Monster. Do I really have to say anything about this one?

Back on the ship a short time later, trouble was brewing. And its name was Dropo.

Uncomfortable seeing the kids locked in

their temporary prison—actually an old bunk room unused thanks to the mandated decrease in minimum crew sizes—Dropo decided to take them on a tour of the ship. After all, how many times does a partial belzoid get a chance to show off how much he knows?

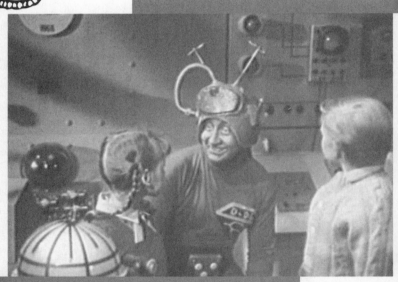

"Okay, Billy and Betty, nobody's here," said Dropo. "Come on in."

"Golly," said Billy. He had thought it was cool when a TWA captain let him wear his hat and gave him a pin with wings on it. This experience was of a different order altogether.

Having shown them the briefing room, the equipment room, the exercise room, the voidatron, and the souvenir shop, the only place left to go was the bridge—which was not only off-limits to prisoners but also to children. In fact, since the initial discovery of the stowaway, it was off-limits to Dropo.

"Now," said Dropo, "I'm not supposed to bring you here. The chief is going to be awful mad if he finds us."

"Boy," said Billy, "wait until the kids at home find out I was in a real Martian spaceship." In a remarkably Dropo-like move, he reached for a switch.

"Careful—don't touch anything," Dropo warned, which is kind of like a flegburn bug warning a basin bat not to krizen. If you know what I mean.

"Now, here," said Dropo, pointing to marvel after marvel—at least to an Earthling—"That's the anti-gravity generator. And these are the retro-rockets."

Dropo, despite his appearance, actually had an advanced degree in thermonuclear navigation.

"Does this light up?" Billy asked, checking out the bulbs on the radar controls.

"Only when radar waves are bouncing off our ship," explained Dropo. "Then we put up this radar screen. Then nobody can find us in space."

See, not only was Dropo brilliant, but he knew how to articulate scientific principles for the masses. Kind of a Carl Sagan type. We watch Carl Sagan's shows. University students drink whenever a primitive scientific error is made. Big bang, indeed.

"Boy, that's pretty sharp," said Billy, impressed by the detail of the radar screen system.

"Yep."

"What's this, Dropo?" asked Betty.

"Oh, that's the elevator signal. That light comes on when someone's coming up from the navigation deck." He didn't say that it was installed by Voldar to prevent anyone walking in while he was looking at inappropriate sites on the Galaxy-wide Web.

As if on cue, the light turned on.

"Somebody's coming up," said Billy, nervously. "We better get out of here."

"No. No. Don't," said Dropo, struggling to remain calm. "There's no time for that. Uh-oh, I'm in trouble. Here, quick! Go in."

He opened the lid to the radar box—the same place he hid during takeoff from Mars—and hustled the children in, closing the lid just in time for the arrival of the landing party.

"Thinking of taking another nap in the radar box, Dropo?" asked Voldar as he entered.

"No, sir," said Dropo, thinking fast—at least by Dropo standards. "As a matter of fact, I was just looking in there to remind myself never to hide there again."

To Dropo, that made sense.

"I bet," said Voldar, master of the witty comeback.

He had just moved to open it, when Rigna announced, "We're approaching the North Pole."

"I can see Santa Claus's workshop," said Father, who, once he got the magnascope working, could play it for all it was worth. "Prepare for landing."

All of which distracted Voldar from the radar box.

"Hargo, set the rocket silencers," said Father. "Dropo, you stay on board and guard those children. They must not leave the ship now."

"Now?" said Voldar ominously. He was always good on ominous. "Or ever?"

"What do you mean, Voldar?" asked Father, who hadn't really thought through what to do with the kids.

"If we take them with us to Mars," he explained, "Santa's disappearance will remain a mystery. No one on Earth will ever know that Santa Claus was kidnapped by Martians."

"Perhaps you're right," conceded Father. "Dropo, get right to those children and don't let them out of your sight, understand?"

"Yes, sir. I understand," said Dropo, uncertain whether to follow Father's order and watch the radar box or to go below where the children were supposed to be. "I'll keep an eye," he assured the rest of the crew, opting for the latter.

Moments later, the ship had landed yet again, this time in the frozen Arctic.

"Secure the ship," said Father. "Lomas, you remain on guard and have the ship ready for immediate blastoff. Rigna, Hargo, Voldar, you'll accompany me. Come, we'll activate Torg."

"Torg? To capture a roly-poly little man like Santa Claus? We don't need Torg."

"We won't take any chances. Come. Nothing can stop Torg."

Bet you're wondering about Torg. Don't worry, you'll experience the terror that is Torg very soon.

The kids had heard the plan. When the coast was audibly clear, they poked their heads out and looked around.

"They're going to kidnap Santa Claus. And us, too," said Betty as she climbed out.

"Not if we can help it," said Billy. "But we've got to get out of here and warn Santa."

Not an easy task. And besides . . .

"What's a Torg?" Betty asked, not really sure if she wanted to know the answer.

"I don't know. But I'm not afraid of it," said Billy. "It's not going to stop us. Come on."

But then an idea. "Wait, Betty," he said, reached back into the box, and pulled a fistful of radar-screen cords from their connections.

"Why did you do that?"

"If this ship should ever leave Earth, we'll have

RADAR BOX

the whole U.S. space force after us," he explained. "Come on."

Quickly, they were on their way down the ladder that extended from the bottom of the ship to the frozen North Pole ground below. They could hear the brisk wind, but nothing seemed to be blowing. Long shadows stretched across the landscape. "Come on, Betty," he encouraged, knowing they had to act fast—not only to find Santa, but to get safely away from the Martians, and to avoid freezing to death.

Through the snow they ran, clearing the landing area just moments before the Martian party descended from the ship's bowels.

7

In Which Betty and
Billy Encounter
a Polar Bear
and an Even
More
Fearsome
Martian
Creation; and Santa
Meets the Martians

"**T**his action must take place swiftly," said Father, at the landing site. "We can't afford to make any mistakes. Hargo, you cover the rear of the workshop. Rigna, Voldar: cover the front entrance. I'll direct Torg."

"Voldar isn't here," noted Rigna, not seeing Voldar coming down the ship's ladder at that very moment.

"Rigna, go up and tell . . . " began Father, but then he saw that his first in command had descended the ship's ladder and finally arrived. "Voldar, this is another one of your delaying tactics. You've been opposing me at every turn. Now I'm warning you, change your attitude."

"You finished . . . Chief?" asked Voldar, smugly, the last word said with a bite.

"Yes I am . . . and you will be, too, if you're not careful."

"Oh, but I am careful . . . Chief. So careful that I looked in on the children before I left the ship."

"You stay away from those children."

"That will be easy to do," Voldar replied. "They've escaped."

"Voldar, if this is your idea of a joke . . . "

LOU HARRY

"Ask Dropo. They overheard our plans. At this very moment, they're on their way to Santa Claus to warn him."

"It's true, Kimar," said Rigna, pointing to the ground. "Their footprints."

"We must stop them," said Father. "Those children mustn't reach Santa Claus. Follow them. I'll put Torg on the trail."

And then Father slowed down his speech, for he was no longer talking to educated, superior Martians. He was talking to . . .

"Torg. Come. Out. Of. The. Space. Ship. Torg. Come. Out. Of. The. Space. Ship."

Desperate times call for desperate measures.

Not far away, the children were running, hands intertwined.

"Billy, I can't run anymore. I'm cold and I'm tired. And it's beginning to snow."

"Please, Betty, try. We've got to warn Santa. We can't stop now. They might catch us."

"Where is Santa?" she asked.

"I don't know. But his workshop must be somewhere around here." Billy was, of course, making the assumption that the Martians had the foresight to land close enough to the workshop to manage a kidnapping but far enough away not to trigger any alarm system that Santa may have installed. Or had his elves install.

Over a snowbank, Billy saw the being at the top of his Beings I Don't Want to See list.

"Betty, look. It's Voldar."

"He's the mean one," she whispered. "The one who doesn't like us." Betty was an astute judge of character.

"Come on," said Billy, not sure where he was leading his sister. But there had to be something . . .

. . . like an ice cave. Perfect. They scurried in just in time to avoid Voldar, blaster in hand.

It didn't take him long to find the trail of the children, who were unaccustomed to being tracked by such an expert hunter. After a few steps in the right direction, Voldar eyed the ice cave suspiciously. Here was a place that a pair of children might hide if . . .

But a distraction appeared . . . a large, furry, powerful distraction the likes of which was never seen on Martian soil (not that Mars has soil, but you get what I mean).

Any Earthling would recognize it as a polar bear. A somewhat emaciated polar bear, but a polar bear nonetheless. One that could knock the antennae off a Martian's head in a single swat—and maybe take the Martian's head with it.

Voldar backed away slowly . . . then ran as fast as his legs could carry him. He may have been evil, but he was also sensible.

After a reasonable wait of a few seconds, the kids peeked out.

"He ran away," said Billy, stunned by their luck. "But, boy, that was a narrow escape."

"Why did he run away?" asked his sister.

"I don't know. . . ."

But then he knew.

"Uh-oh."

The hungry polar bear, apparently tired of chasing Voldar, returned. The children ducked back into the cave and pressed themselves as close to the back wall as they could. The roar of the beast was like nothing they had heard before.

"Get back, Billy," warned Betty.

A giant emaciated paw reached into the cave, its frustrated owner doing everything in its power to reach the cowering youths, for fresh meat didn't come along often in these parts, and elves rarely strayed far from the workshop. Could it be that earlier today the siblings were lounging by their neighborhood lake? Could it be that such a short time ago their worst problem was trying to get a mini hot dog out of the neck hole of Betty's decapitated Barbie doll (don't ask)? Even when the Martians had taken them, the children had never feared for their lives.

But this? What if the creature managed to reach just a few more inches? What if its actions caused the cave to collapse? What if the creature was patient and remained outside until they froze or starved to death?

But even an emaciated polar bear with an odd ridge along his neckline, like the separation line between a mask and the rest of a costume, knows when it's time to give up. Unable to administer even a scratch to the terrified children, the beast withdrew its mitt, growled in frustration, and stepped away from the cave. Besides, the news crew it had attacked earlier in the day had been satisfying enough.

"Don't move, Betty. I'll go take a look," said Billy.

She moved anyway, following her big brother to the opening of the cave.

"It's all right now, Betty, come on," he instructed, aware now that they had two enemies out there in the dark.

"I'm cold," said Betty. "I wish it wouldn't snow."

But Billy saw a silver lining in those storm clouds. "That's the best thing that could happen. It'll cover our tracks and make it hard for the Martians to find us."

"And," added Little Miss Dark Cloud, "it'll be harder for us to find Santa's workshop. I'm scared."

"We'll find it," said Billy. "Which way is north?"

But Billy didn't need a compass or an understanding of the positions of the stars. A glance over the next hill revealed something.

"I see it. I see Santa's workshop!" said Betty, unaware of the effect that snow and cold can have on otherwise textbook vision.

"Where?"

"Right there. See the light?"

Could that be Santa's workshop? Billy wondered. On the video machines, the Claus digs looked more Thomas Kincaid-ish. (On Mars, by the way, the Earthling "painter of light" is all the rage right now. My aunt and my bio-cousin both have extensive collections purchased from smugglers, who make frequent Earth runs to acquire them.)

But something wasn't quite right. The lights should not have been moving. This wasn't Santa's workshop at all. In fact, the lights were moving toward them. They wouldn't learn its name until later, but they were being approached by one of Mars's most fearsome weapons—the creature that had single-handedly put down the riots of Felzar-2, squelched the Brogita Borgita Borg uprising, and developed a needle that would both knit and crochet.

"It's coming toward us," said Betty.

"Betty, that's not Santa's house. Look."

With a fearsome square chest, a fearsome bucketlike head, two lights where a human's eyes would be, and a pair of fearsome dials on his chest indicating who knows what fearsome measurement, Torg worked his way across the frozen terrain, swinging his thing-that-connects-the-laundry-dryer-to-the-wall-like arms as he moved.

"What is it?" asked Betty.

"I don't know."

They froze in terror as Torg approached. The children were defenseless against his mighty gasp as he lifted them off the tundra and awaited orders from his master.

"Good work, Torg," said Voldar, coming over the snowdrift. "Now destroy them. Crush them. Crush them, Torg. Do as I say."

Lucky for them Voldar wasn't Torg's master.

"Voldar, I knew you'd try something like this," said Father, catching up to his renegade compatriot. "I set Torg's controls so that he will obey only me. Release them, Torg."

And he did.

"You were very lucky," Father told the children. "Now don't try to escape again. You may not be so fortunate next time. Rigna, take them back to the ship. Lock them up, and rejoin us."

"You won't get away with this, you . . . " Billy tried valiantly to come up with the most insulting word he could. " . . . you Martian!"

Father had more important matters to contend with than the weak jibes of an Earth child. "The danger grows with every minute," he said decisively. "Let's get Santa Claus and blast off. We'll surround the workshop and send Torg in to get Santa. Nobody is to be harmed unless they get in our way."

"Fine. No one is to be harmed," said Voldar, clearly not thrilled with the plan but understanding the chain of command. That understanding didn't keep him from pondering—and stating aloud—the big question: "What has happened to the great warriors of our planet? Mars used to be the planet of war. Mark my words, Kimar. Your softness will destroy us. Santa Claus. Toys. Games. Laughing children."

"Well, we shall see," said Father, beginning to second-guess his choice of second in command. "But for now, to your posts. Torg, follow me."

The robot followed his master's commands, all the way to the charming cottage that was the above-ground portion of Santa's elaborate workshop. Father could see the elves hard at work. He could see the toys being lovingly produced by hand. And he could smell the holly. He kind of liked the smell of holly. The Martian olfactory system being what it is, holly smelled like what Earthlings would label "new car." Which is one of the reasons why, while our planets can get along, we will never be truly compatible. It's why, even to this day, Martian/human mar-

riages don't work out. They can never get the smell right.

But that's now. This was then. And with three little words, the attack was launched—and those words, I am semi-ashamed to admit, were proclaimed by my father.

"Get him, Torg," he ordered.

The single-minded creation obeyed, walking menacingly toward the door, banging on it, knocking it in, and ducking his head to clear the low opening (this was not a feature on the first two Torg prototypes and many a doorway paid the price).

The elves tried to fight. At least, those who didn't run blindly tried to fight. One even had the presence of mind to take a Santa Slugger wooden baseball bat and attempt to bunt the robot into submission.

"You can't come in here, no one's allowed," said that bold elf. But Torg grabbed him and lifted him up off the ground.

Santa, for his part, was not frightened by the violation of his workshop. "Well, where did you come from?" he said, admiring Torg while disapproving of his actions. "You're the biggest toy I've ever seen."

He laughed and walked around the robot—who for some reason that Martian robotologists are still trying to explain—put down the elf and stood menacingly still.

"And very well made, too," added Santa.

The landing party was justifiably astonished.

"By the great Dog Star," said Father. "Santa's treating him like a toy. Get him, Torg. Grab him."

But Torg didn't move.

"He's become a toy," observed Voldar.

"Rigna, we'll have to get Santa ourselves," improvised Father. "Come on, Voldar."

They burst into the workshop, wielding the blaster.

Again, Santa was nonplussed.

"Heh, heh, what have we here? More toys?"

"Those are Martians," said Winky.

"Santa Claus," Father said, "you're coming with us."

"No, you can't take him now," protested Winky. "It's too near Christmas!" One wonders what he might have said if the Arctic assault had happened in January.

"Quiet, you," ordered Voldar.

"But—"

He never finished the sentence. Voldar squeezed the trigger on the blaster, freezing all the elves in their tracks, and leading one to wonder why the Martians even bothered with Torg in the first place, when such an effective weapon was readily at their disposal. What one might not realize is that there is a cost to operating the blaster: overuse it and you cannot evacuate your bowels for seven moons.

Don't worry, I don't understand the physiomatics of that, either.

"We don't want to hurt you, Santa Claus," said Father, satisfied with the power of the weapon, "so come along quietly."

Santa inspected the frozen elves slowly and deliberately. Long ago, he had sworn to protect them. Now he saw that a jolly laugh and a hearty ho, ho, ho wasn't effective against all weapons—at least, not in the short term. He had assumed, wrongly, he realized now, that the weapons were just modified versions of the Whammo Air Blaster, a great toy that Santa wished he had invented himself. Now it was the device that created the silent shot heard 'round the world. For if this was the start of a war— and for all they knew at the time, it was—then Winky was its Crispus Attucks. Or its Figio Plinkness, depending on which planet you're from. Surely, if Earth won the battle to come, schools and highway rest areas would be named for the brave, frozen elf.

"Why, why did you have to do that to my helpers?" Santa asked.

"It's harmless," explained Father. "It will wear off in a short while."

"Oh. Well, why didn't you say so in the first place?" said Santa, realizing that no matter how things went, the future probably would not hold a Winky Memorial Middle School.

"You come with us," said Father. "We need you on Mars."

Santa stopped to wave a hand in front of Winky's face. The elf stared blankly.

"Are you sure this is harmless?" asked Santa.

But before anyone could answer, Mrs. Claus entered.

"Oh, I never saw such lazy people," she said, giving a clear idea why most of the elves weren't big fans of hers. "Standing around like statues. There's work to be done."

Father and the rest of the Martians knew immediately that they'd have to administer at least one more blast. He squeezed the trigger, rendering Mrs. Claus, for the first time in her life, speechless.

Also motionless, finger pointing accusingly.

"Oh my, oh me, oh my, oh," said Santa, "Mrs. Claus is going to be very angry about this."

"Take him, Torg," ordered Father.

But something strange happened. Or, rather, didn't happen.

"Torg, take him," Father continued. "Obey my command."

But Torg was stubborn. For the first time in his robotic life—well, not exactly life, but you know what I mean—Torg did not follow an order. Something about Santa and the workshop and, perhaps most important of all, the toys made it impossible for Torg to do any harm.

"Forget it, Kimar," said Voldar, who was used to shifting plans based on battlefield conditions. "Rigna was right, he's nothing but a toy now. Best to leave him here."

Santa, knowing not when he would return to his beloved wife—and unsure whether or not, in her present state, she could hear or see him—offered a preemptive apology to his bride.

"Believe me," he said, "I had nothing whatsoever to do with this. You know, my dear, I can't recall a time when you were so silent for so long."

But in his toymaker's mind, he couldn't help thinking how delighted children next year would be if he could come up with a smaller version of Torg— without the ability to cause death and destruction, of course.

"Let's go, old man," said Voldar, grabbing him by the arm.

And with one last disbelieving look at the state of his beloved Mrs. Claus, Santa left the building, leaving his wife and helpers as still as the disobedient robot.

8

In Which Santa Claus Is Kidnapped

"**S**anta Claus Kidnapped by Martians" screamed the front page of the *Daily Tribune.*

"W Zuu I Smutku Narod Polski Zegna Aleksandra Zawadzkiego" screamed the front page of the *Zycie Warszawy.*

"Sempre Grave Lo Stato Di Segni" screamed the front page of *Corriere Della Sera.*

"Critiche le condizioni di Segni con lieve migliora-mamento in serata" screamed the front page of *Giornale Di Sicilia.*

"Martians Kidnap Santa Claus!" screamed the headline of yet another edition of *Daily Tribune,* where one of the headline writers apparently wasn't terribly happy with the cadence of the first headline.

If *USA Today* had been around back then, there would have been a really cool pie chart.

The broadcast outlets were, of course, slower to report the story than the print ones. But soon they were on the case.

"And Mrs. Santa Claus has positively identified the kidnappers as Martians," said the announcer, knowing he should remain objective but thrilled to have some bit of information that perhaps this world crisis might somehow be resolved in Earth's favor.

"Never before in the history of mankind have the nations of the world reacted with such unanimity and cooperation. Tonight, the lights will burn until dawn in the United Nations building as the leaders of the world map a course of action."

And, truly, those lights were on. Petty territorial and economic disputes were put aside. Even those countries that were Martian-like in their failure to embrace Santa Claus understood the magnitude of this event.

"At Cape Kennedy," the reporter continued, "our correspondent interviewed Werner Von Green, the man in charge of America's Star Shot program."

Von Green was an imposing man who, oddly, bore a slight resemblance to Chochem, the ancient one. I've seen pictures. Now that I think about it, I've never seen the two of them in the same room.

"Mr. Von Green, what is the space agency doing about this?" asked the reporter.

"Well, they have mobilized all the men and equipment in our Star Shot project. And we have rushed our astronauts into an intensive program for the final phase of their training. Now, our Star Shot ship is supposed to undergo six months of test flights.

LOU HARRY

But we are going to forget about the testing and go after those Martian monkeys."

At this point, I must object to Mr. Von Green's comments. While anyone reading this document thus far would clearly know that my sympathies lie with Santa, the children, and the people of Earth who must have been terrified at the sudden capture of this most beloved personage, I would be remiss if I didn't chastise the scientist for his planetist comment. Martian monkeys, indeed.

Besides, unlike humans—who bear an evolutionary relationship with monkeys—my people are descended from a common ancestor of Martians and Saturnians. Kind of embarrassing, but true, although there are some Martians who deny the scientific evidence and try to keep this from being taught in public schools. Nonetheless, you'll never hear me make an Earth-monkey joke.

"Isn't that risky?" the reporter asked, referring to the planned rush launch of *Star Shot*.

"Of course it is risky," answered Von Green. "But every one of our astronauts is begging for the chance to go after the Martians. Who wouldn't give everything to bring Santa back to our children?"

I admire that about you Earthlings. When you've got a good thing going—and certainly this Santa

Claus thing was a good thing—you aren't about to let anyone take it away.

Even by rocket.

On the control deck of *Spaceship Number 1*, the crew tried hard not to be overly celebratory. But they knew their mission was complete and that the Earthlings had been pathetic in their defense. In fact, the biggest threat to their mission had been two small children, who were now safely stowed away behind a locked door.

"Earth hasn't reacted yet," said Rigna.

"No radar beams are being bounced off our ship," added Father, proudly. "Looks like we made a clean getaway."

Hargo entered the control room, laughing. Yes, laughing. "Ah, ha-ha."

"How's our captive?" asked Father.

"He's having the time of his life," said Hargo, who, when he wasn't on duty, was running Mars's largest comic book store.

No, that's not out of character for Martians. Our comics are just a little different from yours. For example, they aren't comic.

"He's such a funny little man," said Hargo of his conversation with Santa Claus. "Why, I've only been with him for five minutes and he has me laughing just like an Earthling. Ha-ha-hah-hah."

Rigna looked up from his monitor, amazed. He had roomed with Hargo for sixteen years at the Academy and had never heard the guy laugh.

"What's soft and round and you put it on a stick and you toast it on a fire?" asked Hargo, then remembered another key part of the question. "And it's green?"

"I don't know," said Father. "What?"

Hargo could barely get the answer out. It seemed even funnier in his head than it had when Santa had told him just a few minutes ago.

"A Martianmallow. Ha-ha."

Against their better judgment, Rigna and Father laughed. It felt strange in their throats and in their mouths.

By the way, that Martianmallow joke ended up sweeping Mars. I mean, really sweeping. And it spawned a movement. Within a year after the completion of the Santa Claus incident, Martian jokes were all the self-deprecating rage on my planet.

Not that they were any funnier than Martianmallows.

On the control deck, Voldar looked at the others with his trademark scowl. "That's what you're all becoming," said Voldar. "Martianmallows. Soft. Weak. That old man is a menace."

A short while later, Santa and the Earth children were locked away in Stateroom Number One. Others might have wallowed in the hopelessness of the situation. Not Santa. He had quickly found a kindred spirit in Dropo, the Martian stowaway. Dropo's energy and good nature helped keep Santa's spirits up, and the North Pole resident knew that his primary mission on this fantastic journey was to keep the children from despair.

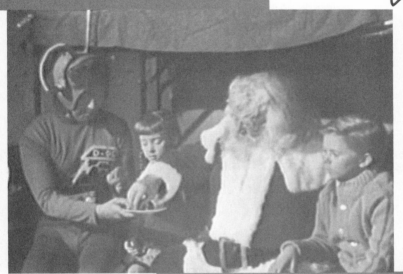

"And it was a very foggy Christmas Eve," he was telling them. "Well, I could barely make out this chimney in the fog. But I found it all right and I started to crawl in. Well, I'll tell you, it was the biggest chimney I'd ever been in. And then suddenly . . . suddenly I realized it wasn't a chimney at all. It was the smokestack of the *Queen Elizabeth!*"

The kids stared at him with the same blank expression as the frozen elves back at the workshop.

"Well, don't you think that was funny?" asked Santa, like a stand-up comic playing in front of a casino showroom filled with blackjack losers.

"Yes, Santa," monotoned the children.

"Well, why don't you laugh?" said Santa, unaccustomed to not being amusing.

"Gee, Santa, it's all our fault," said Billy. "We told them where to find you."

"Oh, balderdash and fiddle-dee-dee, Billy boy, everybody knows where Santa lives. Besides, I always wanted to visit Mars."

"Mommy and Daddy are going to be angry," said Betty, not seeing the face that had just appeared at the barred window.

"You think that's something?" said Santa, clearly with familial issues of his own. "I can just see Mrs.

Claus now. Christmas coming and I'm not there. She'll have a fit."

The thought was funny at first. Then, not so funny.

"Oh me, oh my, oh me," he added.

The door of the cell opened. It was Dropo. In addition to other chores, he was assigned to deliver the prisoners their evening meal.

"Come and get it," he announced. "Dinnertime."

If there's anything that could take Santa's mind briefly away from his wife, it was food.

"Ho, ho. Here's Dropo," said Santa, trying valiantly to share his upbeat mood with the downbeat children. "If I can't cheer you up, Dropo can. He always makes me laugh."

"You'll have a wonderful dinner tonight," said Dropo, pointing to each of the pills in turn. "Soup and beef stew and chocolate ice cream."

"No, thank you, Dropo," said Billy. "I'm not that hungry."

"Come on, Billy," the eager-to-please Martian coaxed.

But Billy wanted no part of it.

"Oh, well, is it all right if I have your chocolate ice

cream?" asked Dropo, who had recently been feeling an inexplicable urge to fatten up.

"Sure," said the children.

"Oh, I just love chocolate ice cream," Dropo said, downing the appropriate pill.

Santa let out the weakest of chuckles. But it didn't prove contagious with the somber children.

"Gee," said Betty, as Dropo left. "Mars must be a terrible place to live. Some chocolate ice cream."

Santa didn't go for the idea either. "Pills for dinner?" he said. "I suppose if a Martian has a headache, he doesn't take pills, he takes chocolate ice cream. Heh, heh."

The children reacted as if he had told them it was time for bed.

"Oh, dear, oh, dear," he said to himself. Tough crowd.

LOU HARRY

9

In Which Our Villain Voldar Hatches an Evil Plot

"**K**imar, look at this," said Rigna. "That small blip is not an asteroid. It's a spaceship and it's on our tail. It's getting closer."

We had a tendency to underestimate our opposition. It's a Martian thing.

"Impossible, Rigna," said Father. "They couldn't have spotted us. We have our radar shield on."

"I know that, sir, but they *are* gaining on us."

"Is it possible that Earth has a secret device that can penetrate our radar shield?" pondered Father.

He didn't ponder that question for long. Voldar, who had been taught from a young age the directive "always check the source of power" opened the radar box and discovered the problem.

"They have a secret device," he said, revealing the disconnected wires. "And his name is Billy Foster. I warned you that these Earthlings were dangerous. They'll destroy us if we allow them. Well, I won't allow them."

And he stormed out.

"I think we underestimate the resourcefulness of these Earth people. Very clever of the boy," reacted Father with some degree of admiration. "Make the repairs, Rigna. I'll take evasive action."

As he did, Voldar was heading for the cell, plot already hatched for how to deal with the young saboteurs.

"Well," he said as he entered, "how are Santa and the little Earthlings? It must be tiresome cooped up in this little room. Say, how would you like to see the rest of the ship?"

"You're not fooling me," said Billy. "You don't like us."

"You're mean," added his sister.

"Oh, come on, now, that's not true," pleaded Voldar. "Why, Santa makes everyone feel good. Even me."

"I don't trust you," said Billy.

"Now, now, Billy boy," said Santa. "That's not the

Christmas spirit. Why, of course, Voldar, we'd love to take the grand tour."

Santa didn't always have the best judgment. Or maybe he just knew that the end was near for all of them. Kind of like Jerry Lewis in *The Day the Clown Cried.* That movie may not have ever been released on Earth, but it made all sorts of top-ten lists here on Mars. Even though, at that time, Martians still didn't do much laughing (except when the Tickle Ray was involved), Jerry Lewis was big box office.

"All right, children," said Santa, ushering them out the door to their first—and, Voldar hoped, last—stop.

"**W**arning," warned the sign, "Check equipment before leaving ship."

That ominous bit of assistance was the most prominent item in the room where Voldar led Billy, Betty, and Santa.

"This," announced Voldar, "is called the . . . "

But Voldar didn't have a chance to complete his sentence. Billy knew.

" . . . air lock."

"That's right."

"Sure," the boy-who-would-be-engineer continued, "this is where you come when you're ready to go out in space. It's airtight. You put on your space suit and go out through that door. When you come back, the door closes and they pump air back into the room through there." He indicated a large-but-not-too-large tube in the back corner behind the door.

"When it reaches the pressure of the rest of the ship," Billy continued, "you can take your space suit off."

"Smart lad," said Voldar, patting the boy on the head.

"Where's the control that opens the door, sir?" asked Santa.

"Not here," said Voldar. "That's on the control deck. You see, once you pull that switch, the warning bell sounds, and in sixty seconds, that door opens."

"That's to give the spacemen a chance to get a final check on their equipment," lectured Billy. "There's no air out in space. If that door were open now, it would pull all of the air out of this room . . . and us with it."

"You certainly know a great deal about space travel, son," said Voldar, honestly impressed.

"He's going to be a spaceman when he grows up," said Betty proudly.

"Maybe sooner than that," said Voldar, quietly pulling the door shut—with himself on the other side.

"Santa, that clock stopped," observed Betty, pointing above the warning sign. She was right.

"Sixty seconds," said Billy. "That must be the door timer."

Billy knew what that meant. He bolted to the other door, where Voldar had slipped out. But he knew what would happen when he tried to open it.

"Santa, he locked us in."

"Oh, I don't think so," excused Santa. "He probably just stepped out for a moment."

Santa's not somebody you'd want to do jury duty with. Yes, we have jury duty on Mars. Three hundred and fifty-nine of us serve on each trial. We do it from home. I'd go into it more, but we're at an exciting part of the story. Remind me later.

"It's locked," said Billy. "I don't trust Voldar. He's not like Kimar and the others."

"I don't like him," Betty shouted extraneously.

"I'm worried, Santa," said Billy.

"Now, now, children. Let's not get excited."

But Santa knew that hope was lost. He knew that while he could get reindeer to fly and knew if kids were bad or good, he did not know how to breathe anything but air.

And at that very moment, Voldar was on the control deck, pulling the switch marked Air Lock Door. It was just a matter of time—sixty seconds, to be exact—before both Earth and Mars would be rid of Santa Claus forever.

In the air lock, the timer moved to fifty-five. Then fifty. Then forty-five.

"It's Voldar," said Billy. "He's going to open the space door."

Billy rushed to the hallway door, banging it with his fists. "Help, Kimar. Kimar, help!"

The banging wasn't helping, but he kept at it anyway because, with all his knowledge of space science, Billy knew there was no way out. At least by banging he felt like he was doing something besides just waiting for his doom.

"Gee, Santa, what are we going to do?" said Billy, stopping his banging long enough to look at the clock. "Once that door opens, we haven't got a chance."

Santa was not ready to give up. While he couldn't bring breathable air into the chamber, and he couldn't seal shut the door to outer space, he could make use of one of his most mysterious and wonderful supernatural skills.

"Where did you say this leads to, Billy?" asked Santa, eyeing the smallish air tube.

On the control deck, Voldar counted down.
Seven.
Six.
Boy, he thought, this is fun.
Five.
Four.
It doesn't get much better than this.
Three.
Two.
I will go down in history as the Martian who saved Mars.
One.
Zero.

On the control deck, the rest of the Martian crew saw the indicator that the air lock door had opened.

"Who's in the air lock?" asked Father.

"No one . . ." said Voldar, " . . . now."

"What's going on, Voldar?"

Before he could get a confession out of Voldar, Father heard the door open and turned to see Dropo rush in.

"Chief, Santa and the children are missing," he said.

Father, knowing only one Martian could be behind such a scheme, grabbed Voldar by the tunic, but was quickly pushed back, an offense beyond offenses.

"Where are they?" demanded Father.

"Drifting around in space," said Voldar, self-satisfied, "along with the rest of the space junk."

And then there was a fight. And that fight might not have looked like much to an Earthling observer, but any Martian would understand its magnitude. First, Martians are forbidden to fight other Martians. Moreover, a subcommander must never, ever lay hands on a commander.

And so when Voldar swung his fist at my father, well, it wasn't just a turning point—it was a point of no return.

And then there were punches. And our equivalent of Earthling karate chops, known as L'ingdar. (Back then, there was a L'ingdar studio in every shopping center. I took L'ingdar for three years and got up to my amber headpiece, but then I got kind of bored with it and joined the local Flexnerball team.)

There was throat grabbing and shaking. There were blows that didn't seem to land but had a powerful effect. And there was Voldar's head being banged against the console.

"Before I'm through with you, Voldar," Father said, "you'll wish *you* were floating around out there in space."

It seemed like nothing short of Voldar's unconscious body could stop the battle.

But sometimes, something unexpected changes things.

In this case, it was familiar laughter. Laughter my father never expected to hear again.

"Heh, heh, heh. Merry Christmas, everyone."

Yes, it was him.

"Santa Claus," said Father, halting the pummeling. "You're alive! I thought you were . . . "

"Well," the great man explained, "when Voldar accidentally left us in the air lock, and then came up here and accidentally threw the door switch, we knew we had to get out of there in a hurry or that would be the end of us . . . accidentally, of course."

Father didn't buy the accidentally, of course.

"So," finished Billy, "we crawled out through the air duct."

"The air duct," said Voldar, still punch-drunk from the fight.

"But the air duct is just a little . . . and you're so big," said Father.

And there was much laughter.

"You're talking to Santa Claus, son," said Santa.

"But how?"

"Well, now, you wouldn't want me to tell my secret, would you?" said Santa, who then noticed that Voldar was lying on the floor.

"Oh, poor, poor man, he's fainted. Just like someone who's seen a ghost."

And there was much hysterical laughing. From Santa. From the children. And from Father, who couldn't wait to get home to his children and show them the infectious pleasure of being near the one and only Santa Claus.

10

In Which Our Villain Escapes

It is a special feeling to come home, wherever in the universe that home may be.

"Begin landing operations," ordered Father, already imagining the faces of his children, well, not exactly lighting up. Their faces never lit up.

"Fire retro-rockets one and two."

"Firing retro-rockets one and two."

"Lower landing legs."

Father turned to his new second in comand.

"Rigna, after we secure the legs, lower the ladder, get Voldar out of the brig, and take him to the counsel room. He'll stand trial immediately."

"Right, Chief."

It was a novelty for Father to have a direct underling who didn't offer a cynical, counterproductive comment in response to every order. He liked it. He could get used to this.

With the pull of a switch, *Spaceship Number 1* had landed.

"Hatch open."

"Ladder down."

"Power off. Ship secure."

Rigna entered the makeshift brig, thrilled with the prospect that he would soon be back with his family. He even allowed himself to sing a chorus of that "Jingle Bells" song that Santa had taught him.

"Merry Christmas, Voldar," he said. "All right, on your feet, come on."

But Voldar wasn't in the brig, on or off his feet. Tied up on the bunk in his place was none other than Dropo.

Once his gag was loosened, Dropo tried to explain the ordeal he had gone through. "I was handing him food pills through the bars and he grabbed my wrist and . . ."

"Shut up, Dropo," said Rigna harshly, for he was beginning to sense the kind of damage that Voldar could do—especially now that he had nothing to lose. "Kimar?" Rigna said. "Come in quickly. Kimar?"

"Yes, Rigna," said his leader.

"Voldar has escaped," reported Rigna.

"What?"

"He's gone."

"That can only mean trouble," said Father. "Put a constant guard on Santa and the Earth children. Voldar will be back."

LOU HARRY

11

In Which Santa Claus Lands on Mars and Makes the Martians Laugh

In the corridor of our Martian home, Mother was adjusting the scentiquitor, trying to find a perfect balance of sweet and savory. Then she tried to clear dust off an original M'scowkdfljke sculpture that she had bought on the Martian Shopping Network. She had gone on an MSN kick a few quadrains ago and we still have four-dimensional storage units filled with stuff that Mother swore she would regift.

The sculpture was, of course, self-dusting and so her work was totally unnecessary. But what she was doing really had nothing to do with scentiquitor adjusting or with sculpture dusting. It had to do with nervously waiting for her husband to return from his potentially dangerous mission. For who knew what to expect from a planet where people chewed bubble gum?

Bomar and I were nervous, too.

"Mother, is Father here yet?" my brother asked, for what we knew was the fifth time that spendot unit.

"No, Bomar, I'll call you as soon as he arrives."

"Is Dropo coming back too?" I asked.

"Yes, Girmar. Now go back to your studies."

We left, downhearted. And because we had been sent from the room, we missed Santa's arrival.

And Father's. He entered just moments after we left.

"Oh, Kimar," said my mother, more concerned with the safe return of her husband than with the strange man in the red suit he was supposed to have acquired. Father hastened to her and, without a word, rubbed his nose on her forehead, which is fine in private but is kind of embarrassing when they do it in front of other people. I mean, get a room.

"Are you alone?" Mother asked.

"No," he said, and turned just as Dropo brought in the Earth children. Billy was still wearing his hat. Betty had kept her scarf intact.

"Earthlings," Father added, as if Mother couldn't tell what the antenna-less creatures were. "Billy and Betty."

Mother stooped to their level, touching Billy's arm and face in a way that signaled that mothers are alike everywhere in the galaxy (except for certain parts of Neptune, where they behave more like uncles). She then tilted her forehead toward them and, as Dropo had taught them back on the ship, they each leaned forward to connect. "It's like a handshake," Dropo had explained. "Only without hands and without so much shaking."

"Welcome to our home," said Mother. Mother was always at her best when there was company in the house. Once, I brought home my entire farcheck troupe from sand hockey camp, and they ended up staying through Pilox Day.

"There's someone else, too," said Dropo, as if a

pair of Earth children wasn't enough. "Come on. Come on in."

And then there was that laughter. And that laughter came from a man who clearly was very comfortable walking into strange households as if he belonged there.

LOU HARRY

"Lady Momar," said Santa, bowing as low as his ample stomach would allow. "I'm not accustomed to entering people's homes through the door. But you have no chimney."

It was a joke, but surprisingly, Mother got it. Pretty good for someone who hadn't heard a joke in decades. She does have five advanced degrees, four of them in dead languages, so she's no slouch in the brains department. Still, brains and comedy don't always mix, as I later learned from watching the antics of an apparently half-human/half-vegetable Earthling known as Carrot Top.

"Welcome, Santa Claus," said my mother, meaning it. "We hope you'll make the children on Mars very happy."

"I'll try, dear lady," he said. "I'll try." Not that he had to. Technically, he was a prisoner here. He could just clam up and refuse to ho, ho, ho. He could cause major trouble by going in the opposite direction and making things miserable—scaring the children with tales of elf torture and reindeer attacks. But Santa was being a model prisoner, requiring no restraints or drawn weapons to keep him in line. Like Alec Guiness in *The Bridge on the River Kwai*. Only not so British-y.

Santa took her hand, asking, "Where are they?"

Apparently Santa gets antsy if he's only around people over six and a half micronoms tall.

"Well, we'll start with my youngsters," said Father. "How are they, Momar?"

"The same," she said. "Quiet, remote, and very unhappy. They're inside, studying."

"Well," said the man in the red suit, "let old Santa say hello to them. And I'm sure these children would like to meet them."

"I'll tell them they're here," said Father, ever the genial host. Funny, no. Genial, most definitely. And he could dance, too, but that's really not important unless you decide to adapt my story into a musical for your Broadway. After all, you seem to have had much success with *The Producers* and *Hairspray* and this Monty Python thing. And none of those have the inherent drama and pathos as this story. Think of the big number in Santa's workshop. The dancing polar bear? Mandy Patinkin as Voldar?

Am I detecting some interest?

We'll talk later.

Anyway, when Father came in, we were lying on the study cubes, picking up a few extra minutes of galactic navigation theory. "*Y* over 5 *pi r* squared to determine the correct orbit from Mars to Jupiter, traveling along vector k through the 17th quadrant at the power of 12 megatrons."

We were working on a little math problem. Bomar kept messing up, accidentally factoring in vector j instead of vector k. It's been decades since I made that kind of childish mistake, but I guess you have to get used to it with Martian boys, who have never been as strong in math and science as Martian girls.

"Father," I said, when I saw his cape-enswirled self enter the study. "Father, we missed you." And I meant it. Mother just isn't as good with the sleep mister as he is.

"I missed you too," he said. "Children, I brought some visitors from Earth." He turned to the door and called, "Will you come in please, children?"

Frankly, we had no idea what he was talking about. Visitors? From Earth? The last time he brought a visitor from another planet, it was a very smelly diplomat from the outer rim.

But these two creatures looked nothing like diplomats. They were just two antenna-deprived, pale Earthlings.

"Billy and Betty," said Father, "this is Bomar, and Girmar."

"Hi," said Billy, reaching out his gloved hand.

We didn't quite know how to take that gesture. We were young. Bomar just stared at it.

"There's nothing in it," he said. "What are you giving me?"

"My hand. To shake," said the Earth boy.

Billy? What kind of name is that? I wondered. But

I knew it was not my place to make fun of the names of another species. And that's when I noticed that Father and Mother had slipped out, leaving us alone with these two odd Earthlings.

Bomar shook his hand. Over and over again. Now that I understand Earth customs a little better, I understand how silly that must have seemed. But the Earth boy and girl took it in stride.

"I'm ten," said Billy. "How old are you?"

"I'm ten," said Bomar, assuming that he was talking about macroyears. "And Girmar's eight."

"So's my sister," said Billy.

Any Martian could tell you, the odds of such a random meeting between like-aged pairs is well into the thousands-to-one. I was going to do the calculation, but Father had more news in store.

"We have another Earth person who wants to meet you," he said, sweeping back into the study room.

Then he ushered in our third visitor, and we heard that laughter. Father ducked back outside to join Mother, and listened carefully for our reaction.

You should understand here that we had absolutely no idea what Father's mission had been. We'd assumed it was just another round of asteroid clearance. Mother did not share with us that Father

was on a mission to kidnap Santa Claus. Later, she told me that she feared our disappointment, should the goal of the mission not be achieved. Or should Father meet his fate at the hands of irate elves. They are rumored to be brutal when provoked.

So we stared, for surely this could not be really happening. The man from the North Pole, here on Mars?

He kept laughing.

And the Earth children laughed with him.

And then the sound of my laughter joined the cacophony. And my brother's.

Why were we laughing? I don't know. No joke had been uttered, no sight gag presented, no piece of sports equipment had come into contact with a sensitive part of the anatomy. Yet my large-toothed brother and I were giggling as if wrestling with a Tickle Ray.

"What's that?" Dropo asked Mother and Father, as all three eavesdropped at the door.

"They're laughing," Father said. "Bomar and Girmar, too."

"They've never laughed before," marveled Mother.

"Come," said Father, pointing at the door to make it open. Mother entered, then Father.

And Dropo, well, he waited a moment before he came in. Because he was so happy, he had to do a little dance.

12

In Which
Voldar Hatches
Another Evil
Plot; and the Earth
Children Feel
Homesick

lsewhere on Mars, Voldar and his not-exactly-
friend Stobo were stewing in their makeshift
hideout, a cave in the side of the crater of
Muldun where, as young boys, the two would plot
the overthrow of the Martian government.

"Me, Voldar. Hiding in a dirty cave like a speckled

Mars worm," he grumbled, as Stobo warmed his hands by a carbolic fire. "Oh, Kimar will get his. I'll find a way," and he reached his hands out as if to strangle the Martian leader.

"That's easy. Let's get rid of his fat little friend in the red suit," offered Stobo, who was never big on original ideas.

"Fool. That's suicide," stated Voldar, swatting at Stobo. "Santa Claus is under constant guard. We couldn't get within twelve feet of him without being disintegrated. But I have other plans."

Although they both knew that plans needed to change based on circumstances—such as a noise outside.

Stobo jumped from his spot by the fire and looked to the entrance. "Someone's approaching the cave," he said.

"Who?"

"It's me," said Shim, another of Voldar's henchmen. They were officially henchmen now. Before Voldar's split with Father, they were just known as personal assistants.

"All right. Turn off the nuclear curtain," ordered Voldar. The nuclear curtain was the thing for keeping out intruders. Stobo hastened across the cave to the control panel, where a few twists and turns of the knobs and levers negated the invisible field that covered the entrance.

"All clear, Shim, enter."

Shim had barely taken a few steps into the cave

when Voldar grabbed him by the scruff of the neck. "What did you find out?"

"The toy shop is operating full blast," reported Shim. "No one suspects me. So I sneaked down and took a good, long look. It's nothing like the one on Earth. No one is sawing or hammering. Kimar's built a mechanized assembly line for the old man. Toys are rolling off by the second. This planet will be flooded with toys."

For Voldar, it was a nightmare worse than the prospect of an all-comedy cable channel on the video machine. Toys? Everywhere? How will studying compete with such distractions? What will happen if a neighbor kid throws a ball into his yard? Who will clean up the sidewalk chalk?

But while Voldar was stewing, Shim's face had broken into a blissful grin.

"You know, they've got one little toy," said Shim, as Stobo looked on, fascinated. "It's the cutest thing. It's just a coiled spring. And it goes down steps all by itself. I was tempted to steal one. I'd like to fool around with the thing and . . . "

He was brought back to his senses by the sound— and the pain—of Voldar's hand smacking him.

"Toys! The decay is setting in. It's even affecting

you," said Voldar, who remembered how tough Shim used to be in tight situations. If the mere presence of toys could affect a warrior like Shim in such a pronounced way, what was to become of the rest of the populace? "Soon all the Martians will be blithering idiots. We've no time to lose. We must go into action."

He knew what Shim was thinking.

"Now, we cannot eliminate Santa Claus. But we can discredit him. Make him a laughingstock throughout Mars. Come on," he said, pulling them together for a huddle. "Listen carefully. The workshop closes at ten o'clock. The guards will be at Kimar's house guarding Santa Claus. Now this is what you'll do, see, you'll . . . "

In the newly built toy factory, the kids were hard at work, but enjoying every minute of it. How many children get to be an integral part of the team at Santa's workshop, even if the toys they worked on were to be distributed to Martian children?

"Hi, Billy," said Dropo as he entered the workshop. "Everything okay?"

"Gee, Dropo," the Earth boy said, "everything's great."

"Santa, look, hundreds of thousands of letters from all over Mars," said Dropo.

To meet the demand, dolls were steadily rolling off the assembly line. Along with toy guns. Games, puzzles, action figures, spaceships, fruitcakes . . .

And the children, Martian and Earthling, checked them off, making sure that each request was being met.

"Two dolls," read Betty, and Santa jiggled the appropriate toggle switch.

"Two dolls," he repeated. "Yes."

And almost instantaneously, the "doll" window opened on the toy-making machine and a beautiful new, pink-clad doll emerged, just waiting for a little child to love it. And another followed, dropping to join its sister on the conveyor belt.

"Three baseball bats," read Betty, moving ahead to the next order.

"Three baseball bats," Santa repeated, not questioning what some kid would be doing with three baseball bats. He pushed a button and three emerged from the "bat" window. Now, you might wonder how a machine could be created in a single factory that had enough chutes and windows to accommodate every child's toy needs. During the brief construction period (which lasted the two days after Santa and company had arrived on Mars), Father wondered about that, too, and asked Santa about that very matter. Santa explained his theories of efficient use of elf labor, how the more segmented a product line becomes, the more difficult and costly it becomes to fulfill. He also explained the efficiencies of farming out the labor on those toys that required molded plastic or special licensing. Santa had discovered the value of such outsourcing years ago—along with the benefits of alternate distribution. The reindeer especially appreciated how many of Santa's deliveries were now being shipped through the U.S. Postal Service.

The rest, he and the elves made by hand.

And while he appreciated the remarkable toy production system that Father had created, Santa couldn't hide his disappointment in the way the process marginalized him.

"Look at me, Santa Claus, the great toymaker, pressing buttons," he muttered to himself. "That's automation for you. Technology. Oy. Well, that's enough for today."

He rose from his seat, stood at the center of the workshop, and bellowed for all to hear: "Let's close up shop."

"Okay, Santa," said the obedient children, who would have happily stayed for another shift.

"We sure did a lot today," said Dropo. "A lot of toys came off the line today, Santa."

On his way out, Santa stopped to pick up a garment hanging by the door.

"Pretty nice, eh?" he said, aware of Dropo's admiring gaze. "Lady Momar made it for me." It was a new Santa suit, which would allow him to get his original dry-cleaned.

"Can I try it on, Santa?" asked Dropo.

"Heh, heh. Don't be silly, Dropo. This would never fit you.

"Why," he added, patting Dropo on the stomach, "you'd have to fatten up first."

Santa laughed. So did the kids, who followed him out.

But Dropo was starting to formulate an idea.

Back at our home, we escorted Santa in through the main portal to the anci-room, where Mother and Father were tinkering with more objects—but not ones that Mother had bought on MSN. These were unusual Earth toys from Santa's workshop and factory.

"Well, there's another day gone," said Santa. "You know, as they say on Earth, another day, another dollar."

Which they do say on Earth, but since Santa didn't accept money for his toys—or for their delivery—I didn't really see what he meant by that. But ours is not to reason Santa, I suppose.

"Well, hello, Santa," said Father. "How are you feeling today? Tired?"

"No. No. I'm not tired," said Santa. "But my finger is."

The Earth children braced for a "pull my finger" joke. And why shouldn't they? They had uncles.

But Santa was above such things. He was too concerned about the finger itself and what it said about the industrialization process. "It's been pressing buttons all day long," he said of his digit. "Heh, heh, heh. Well, I think I'll be going, and put my finger to bed."

"Here, children, here's your milk," said Lady Momar, handing over pills to the kids. "You can play for half an hour and then you have to go to bed."

"Daddy, may we watch the Earth program?" I asked.

"Certainly, dear," said Father. "But only for half an hour. Billy? Betty? Don't you want to watch the Earth program?" asked Father.

"Oh, no, sir," said Billy, shuffling his feet. "We're not interested in Earth programs. I'm going to sleep. Good night."

"Me, too," said Betty, as if anyone expected an independent thought out of her.

"Just a moment," Father said, trying to push for more information. But Betty interrupted.

"Good night, Mr. Kimar. Good night, Lady Momar."

"Just a moment, children," Kimar persisted. "Are you feeling well?"

"Oh, we feel fine, sir," said Billy. "Good night."

"Good night," added Betty.

"Has someone been mistreating you?" asked Father, stopping the two children as they attempted to walk away.

"Oh, no, sir," said Billy, wondering when this green guy would get the hint that they just didn't want to talk about it. "You and Lady Momar have just been swell to us. Good night."

They finally got out of the room, leaving Dropo shaking his head and Kimar baffled.

"What could it be, Momar?" asked Father. "They're behaving the way our children used to behave."

"Can't you tell?" she asked him, since he usually seemed as insightful as Chochem, only without the smell. "They're homesick. They miss their parents. Their friends."

She stared down at the doll in her hand. How did that get there?

"Kimar, you must send those children back," she added definitively.

Father knew he couldn't answer while continuing to look into her eyes. He broke from her gaze and stared off, knowing that resistance was futile. "Impossible," he said, but with little authority. For Father was as much in Lady Momar's control as Santa was in Mrs. Claus's. Some things, it seems, are alike just about everywhere in the galaxy.

13

In Which the Dim-witted Dropo Comes Up with an Ingenious Plan

Now, it should be said that Dropo was not exactly a hefty man. Sure, he could stand to lose a few pounds to obtain his optimal body mass, but when you're trying on a Santa suit, "optimal body mass" is a very relative thing.

The pants of the Santa suit hung on him by a pair of suspenders. Of course, Lady Momar hadn't made the suit for him. She'd made it as a backup for Santa.

Still, he liked the feel of these pants. More importantly, he was sure he would like the effect the full Santa suit would have when he wore it. He had tried other professions—crime-scene cleaner, caricaturist, spleek farmer—but what could be more satisfying than bringing happiness to children?

To get to that point, though, there was preliminary work to be done. Gastronomic work.

"Santa says I've gotta fatten up," Dropo said to himself as he studied the pill bottles he had bought to help facilitate this transformation. Malted milk was the first step, and he said those words reverentially as he popped the pill.

He could almost feel the calories go directly to his thighs.

The next: " . . . chocolate cake."

Down went a handful of pills, but he was just getting warmed up.

" . . . banana split."

That one was good.

Next?

" . . . Mmmm. With whipped cream."

Another pill.

He checked the mirror again, pulling the suspenders out and seeing how much more work he had to go.

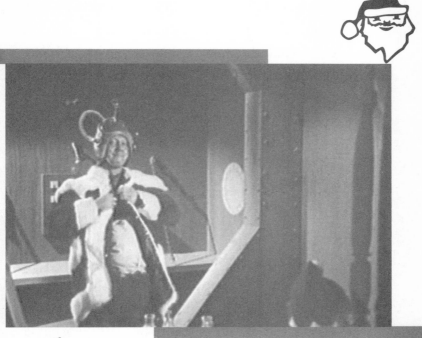

But this method, he knew, would prove too frustrating. At this rate, he would have to wait seven Septobers before he could take off in his sleigh pulled by eight . . . hmmm, he'd have to think about what indigenous Mars creatures could pull it. Surely, Earth reindeer wouldn't be able to make the journey—and wouldn't survive the Martian atmosphere.

They would have to be photogenic as well. Nobody would welcome a sleigh pulled by Verokan knife-birds.

And they ought to be silent. Because apart from some jingling bells and a ho, ho, ho or two, Christmas toy delivery was really a stealth mission.

But all that was irrelevant if he couldn't fill the suit.

Out of the corner of his eye, reflected in the mirror, he saw the answer. In fact, he had been resting on it just a few short hours ago.

Dropo grabbed the pillow, nearly tripping as he did. Then gleefully shoved it into his pants, checking out his personage in the mirror as he did. Getting there. Getting there.

The heavy red coat was next. He slid his arms into the sleeves without removing his eyes from the mirror. Could this be the same Dropo who, in the fractal school yearbook mind chip, was voted Most

Likely to Cause an Unwanted Disruption? Yes, it was. And soon things were going to be very, very different.

Now for the buttons, and a quick look in the mirror to make sure his butt didn't look too big.

And then the beard—the mound of fluffy white that clearly differentiated him from his fellow Martians. For no Martian but the ancient ones sported white facial hair.

He hoped they wouldn't perceive this as disrespectful.

No, how could they? This was all in the spirit of Christmas. And from what Kimar had said, Chochem was the one who got this mission rolling in the first place.

"Now I'm Santa Claus," Dropo said. "Ho, ho, ho." Only it kind of sounded like "who, who, who."

So he put on his hat—not an easy task when you have a metal helmet that carries your antenna and brain fluid—and tried it again. "Ho, ho, ho." Which sounded more like "how, how, how."

This wasn't going to be as easy as it looked.

Dropo took a deep breath, concentrated like he'd never concentrated before (which, to be honest, wasn't saying much), and said, "Ho, ho, ho, Merry Christmas, everyone." And it sounded honest and bold and right and good.

"Ho, ho, ho," he continued, trying to think of other words and phrases the real Santa had said. Then he remembered. Santa had a thing about his finger.

"My finger," Dropo said, believing he was doing a pretty decent Santa impression. "*My* finger isn't hurt. I think I'll go down to the workshop and make some more toys. Ho, ho, ho."

And he started singing "Jingle Bells," a song Santa had taught him. It concerned a group of people entertaining themselves while traversing a field. I would share the words with you but I cannot, due to the risk of some archaic Earth legal concept known as copyright infringement.

The rhythm of that song put a new spring in his step. If his fellow Martians had thought he was enthusiastic before, they'd be amazed to see and hear the new Dropo.

14

In Which Voldar and His Henchmen Wreak Havoc on Santa's Martian Toy Workshop

Before Dropo could get to the workshop, three shadowy figures entered through its unlocked door. One of these shadowy figures was carrying a giant wrench while another shined a big red flashlight on the newly rebuilt machines.

"There it is," said one, spotting what he was looking for—a sign that read "Caution: Controls."

"Shhh."

One of the shadowy figures dropped a bag on one of the other shadowy figure's feet. Then all the shadowy figures bumped into each other and pushed one another and shushed one another in the dark. As

LOU HARRY

they stumbled around and made funny noises, they resembled the Earth trio known as the Three Stooges, only not funny.

Martian girls, by the way, are said not to appreciate Moe, Larry, and Curly—as the Earthling Stooges are called—but I've always been a big fan. Although I don't care for Shemp. In all my research into the matter, I have yet to find a human or Martian who preferred Shemp to Curly. It is comforting to know that some things are universal.

"Shim, hold the light," said Voldar, who then slapped Stobo on the head when the light wasn't taken. "Hold the light," he repeated.

Voldar removed the "Caution: Controls" panel, revealing a maze of wires and computer chips. A toy factory may seem like a simple thing, but it really requires an elaborate series of processes that I can't begin to explain to the backward minds of Earthlings. No offense.

"Ah, this is going to shake them up. These toys will never be the same again," said Voldar, who quickly twisted and turned the proper pieces in a plan inspired by what Billy did to the radar box back on *Spaceship Number 1*.

Voldar slammed the panel door, then tried to shush it. Then he was shushed by Stobo, then by

Shim, then by himself. It was one, big shush-a-palooza. And then . . .

What?

How do I know all of this without being there?

Because . . . I conducted extensive interviews with the participants, that's why. They are all alive and . . . wait . . . by asking that, you are implying that I might be making some of this up. That it didn't happen? Is that what you're saying? Because if that's what you're saying, I could stop right here and not finish the story. It's hard enough keeping Shim and Stobo straight and remembering who was where, when. I was younger then. And I didn't see everything. It's not like I was somewhere in a tree. But I know what happened. I know. So if you want to know, you have to let me tell the story.

And give me a snack cake. Can I have a snack cake? If I can't have a snack cake, I'm not going to finish. I'm done. You'll never know what happened to . . .

Yum. Thank you. There are few things on Earth better than snack cakes.

Where was I?

Oh, yes, the panel was now closed, with no sign of the tampering.

"Someone's coming," said Stobo. "Quick, down."

It was Dropo, fully decked out in Santa garb, singing "Jingle Bells" and dancing as he thought of the pleasure he would have turning on the toy-making machine and using his unhurt finger to push the buttons. Santa will be pleased, he thought, and pleasing Santa was almost as much fun as pleasing children.

"What a break," said Voldar, clearly in need of some laser eye surgery. "It's Santa Claus." Anyone not blinded by hatred would have known that it wasn't Santa.

"With no guard," said Stobo who, by the way, bore a passing resemblance to Jamie Farr, of your Earth series *M*A*S*H*.

The intruders showed their flashlight into his eye, stopping him in his jovial tracks.

"Oh," was all Dropo could say.

"Throw him into the cave," said the villains.

And they did. And in the cave, they continued their insults as Dropo cowered, trying to keep his face covered. For who knew what fate would befall him if they discovered that he was not their intended victim?

"Now, stay put, my fat little friend," said Voldar.

"Hey, Santa, how do you like this toy?" asked Stobo, showing Santa his weapon.

"My friend asked you a question," pushed Shim. "Answer him."

Wisely, Dropo only said, "Ho, ho, ho."

"Quiet," said Voldar. "Put on the nuclear curtain."

Shim twisted the proper knobs, activating the security screen that guarded the entrance to the cave.

"Tomorrow marks the end of Operation: Santa Claus," declared Voldar, "and Mars returns to normal. Ha-ha!"

Dropo sat on the rock in despair. For how could he, the lowly son of Krakenfen welders, single-handedly battle Voldar, the mad genius behind the Desososo conquests? But there had to be something he could do. There just had to be.

Elsewhere on Mars, Dropo's disappearance was once again the subject of discussion. Although, since Dropo had a habit of disappearing, it was not treated as a major problem.

"Dropo. Dropo, you rascal. Where are you?" called Lady Momar. "Dropo?"

But then, other matters became more pressing. "Children," she said, "breakfast is ready."

"Good morning, dear," said Father.

"Kimar," she said. "I can't find Dropo. And his bed hasn't been slept in."

"What's he up to now?"

It was a question they had asked many times. Answering it usually required some search time. They would first check the . . .

But then Santa arrived.

"Good morning! Good morning, Lady Momar," he said, bowing, then remembering what he needed to say, "Oh, my extra suit—the one you made for me—is missing. I'm sure I brought it back from the toy shop last night."

What did you say?

Why did my mother make Santa a fake beard, when he already had a beard?

Well, maybe my mother thought Santa might need an extra beard. How should I know why she made a fake one to go with Santa's extra suit? . . .

Yes, I know, if there wasn't a fake beard, then Dropo's costume would never have been able to work . . . I know. Mom just did things like that sometimes. She was always making fake beards. I mean it. She made fake beards for everyone. We were lousy with fake beards. I'm surprised she didn't make one for you. Now, can I get back to the story?

Thank you.

"That's two things that are missing," said Father. "Your suit and Dropo."

"What? What? Oh . . . That explains it. When you find my missing suit, you'll find Dropo inside it. He's out someplace playing Santa Claus."

"I'll take care of him," said Father, trying to think of the appropriate punishment for impersonating a mythic figure.

"Oh, no, no. Now, let him have his fun," said Santa, not interested in pressing any charges. "He's probably at the toy shop making toys. He loves it."

"Children, will you please hurry," prodded Lady Momar. "Breakfast is ready."

"Yes, if you don't hurry, your breakfast will get cold," said Santa, holding up a jar of pills. "Ha-ha-ha."

Santa loved his food pill jokes.

As soon as he entered the toy factory for the day's work, Santa called for his new friend. "Dropo, we're here."

"Maybe he's hiding, Santa," I suggested. It was just a thought. I'd played hide-and-ride-and-glide with him before.

"Oh, playing hide-and-seek, eh? All right, Dropo, here we come, ready or not. He, he, he."

"He's not here, Santa," concluded Billy.

"Oh, well, he'll turn up. Let's get started."

Santa turned on the machine, which did not require any warm-up time. Nothing on Mars required warm-up time. That's another fundamental superiority of the Martian culture over the Earth culture: preheating, for us, is a thing of the ancient past. We mock it the way your people mock muttonchop whiskers.

"Ready? Okay," said Santa, comfortably settled in his command seat. "Let's get started."

"One teddy bear and one doll," read Betty from the master naughty-or-nice list. She was a very good reader for an Earth child.

"One teddy bear and one doll," repeated Santa, pushing the appropriate buttons.

Since this was to be the first toy off the line that

morning, Santa shifted into quality-control mode, stopping the machine. In the days since the toy machine was reconfigured (it had originally been used for the creation of tires for craterbikes), there had not been a single flaw with any of the 47,392 toys created. A pretty solid record. Still. Santa knew that as soon as he stopped checking his creations, that's when quality would suffer.

If not sooner.

"Santa, something to see," shouted Bomar. "Look!"

"The doll has a teddy bear head," I declared, "and the teddy bear has a doll head."

Bomar held them up to show that I was right.

"I can't understand it," he said. "Let's try it again. What's next, Betty?"

"One baseball bat," she said.

But it wasn't a baseball bat that emerged through the bat chute. It was some twisted hybrid of a baseball bat and a tennis racquet.

"A baseball tennis rac . . . well, I, this will never do," understated Santa. "The machine isn't working right. Oh dear, what else, Betty?"

"Toy train," she read. Back then, apparently, children only requested one item for Christmas.

"A toy train. Well, all right. Here."

He pushed the appropriate button. A toy dropped into the bin.

Bomar brought over the result. So horrible was it that Santa didn't even let us look at it. I never got around to asking Bomar what it was. Next time I see him, I will.

"What?" said Santa with dismay. "Why, this

doesn't make sense. Well, this never happened when we made toys by hand. Something very strange is happening here. Bomar, I think we'd better call your father."

Bomar stepped back and hit the "Dad" button on his personal transmitter. Bomar didn't like to use it, seeing it as a sign of weakness. The last time he hit the "Dad" button was when, well, it's a long, embarrassing story.

"Father, this is Bomar."

"Yes, Bomar."

"Father," he said, "we're in the toy shop. Dropo isn't here. And there's something wrong with the toy machine, too."

"I'll be right over."

Meanwhile, Voldar was ready for the next phase of his plan. "Time to go," he said. "Shim, wake up." Shim seemed to have caught Dropo's sleep disorder.

"I still think you're making a mistake," said his sleepy partner in crime. "It's too dangerous walking right into the enemy camp."

"Kimar and his men wouldn't dare lay a finger on us," said Voldar. "Not while we're keeping Santa Claus a hostage. Now, if we're not back in three hours, you know what to do. All right, Shim, open the nuclear curtain."

Before leaving with Stobo, Voldar turned back to who he thought was Santa. "Just a word of warning," Voldar said. "If you've got any big ideas, forget 'em. If you walk through that nuclear curtain, you'll be disintegrated just like that."

And he snapped his fingers. Martians are great at snapping their fingers. We can do it not just with our thumb and middle finger but also with any two fingers and any two toes. You really should see it.

Dropo watched carefully as Shim pulled the switch that turned on the nuclear curtain.

Father was not happy with what he found at the toy shop.

"Sabotage. Somebody switched all the wires. Dropo's gone. Your suit is missing. And now this machine has been sabotaged. Put it all together and it spells Voldar."

"He was here," Santa said, working out the puzzle in his head and concluding what Father already knew. "And he thought Dropo was me."

"He's got Dropo," said Father, "and I'm going to find him."

"Ohhh, Dropo," said Santa, worried.

Father bolted from the toy shop to prepare for a citywide Martian hunt the likes of which hadn't been seen since Apsapdap the Intruder escaped from Felper's Dune.

15

In Which Our Heroes Engage in a Fierce Toy Battle in Santa's Martian Toy Workshop and Save the Day

But Father didn't go far before he ran into Voldar and Stobo.

"Surprised to see us?" asked Voldar smugly.

"You're under arrest, Voldar," said Father, aiming the blaster at his former first officer.

Voldar laughed. Not a Santa "come join me in merriment" laugh but a Voldar "I've got you beat and you don't even realize it" laugh. Stobo tried laughing along, but Voldar smacked him in the head.

"Stop playing with toys," Voldar said to Father, trivializing the blaster that he himself was instrumental in developing. "Put it away, Kimar. We have a weapon that's much more potent than that."

He didn't give Father much of a chance to imagine what that could be.

"As you may know, we are holding Santa Claus hostage. One false move and your little ho-ho-ho man will be destroyed."

Stobo laughed. Not a Santa "come join me in merriment" laugh or a Voldar "I've got you beat and you don't even realize it" laugh, but more like an "I've fallen out of a rocket and landed on my head" laugh.

Father ignored the sidekick and considered his options. As much as he would have taken pleasure in terminating the mutinous Voldar right then and there, Father knew that such action would invalidate all the risk he took in kidnapping Santa Claus in the first place.

And maybe, he began to think, the kidnapping itself was not the right thing to have done. After all, what Chochem had actually said was . . .

But there was no time to second-guess the mission. There would be time for that later . . . if Santa could be saved.

Santa. He had to think of Santa.

"All right," said Father. "What do you want, Voldar?"

"These are our terms," he said, pausing only to smack Stobo in the head one more time. "First, destroy the toy machine. Second, we will release Santa Claus if you promise to send him and the Earthlings back to their planet. Third, no more joy-through-toys nonsense on Mars."

Joy through toys. If we were on Earth and I had a degree in marketing, I'd consider that as a T-shirt.

Father didn't like taking orders from Voldar. At the same time, though, he tried to imagine the fallout if something dire should happen to Santa Claus. Not only would the children of Mars be devastated, but Earth would surely launch an attack. Oh, Mars would win. There was no doubt of that. But the damage to both sides would be severe.

What am I thinking, Father reminded himself.

Voldar doesn't have the real Santa—Voldar just has Dropo! All of a sudden, the situation looked significantly brighter.

Although he already knew he had to keep him safe, he was beginning to see that crazy old Dropo might have a true calling here on the red planet.

"Well?" said Voldar.

"Well," said Father, "you win."

He offered his arm and Stobo shook it.

Father turned to go, waiting just enough time for dramatic effect—and long enough to suppress his smile at how Voldar was falling into his trap.

"Are you sure you have Santa Claus?" Father turned and asked.

"You *know* we have him."

"You mean you *had* him."

And Father opened the door.

The two evil Martians—well, the one evil one and the other henchman-y one—stepped forward, then reeled back in surprise at the real Santa, standing right in front of them.

"How did he get out of the cave?" asked Stobo.

"Shim. That idiot," shouted Voldar, blaming the obvious one and missing out on his own colossal blunder: he never had the real Santa in the first place.

"And how did he get here so, so, so fast?" asked Stobo, spotting a problem with Voldar's theory.

"Santa Claus has powers that you don't know about," said Father, grooving on the improvisational aspects of this turnabout. "All right, arms up."

And their hands shot up.

While keeping an eye on the duo, Father used his antenna to call the loyal members of his team. "Rigna. Hargo. Lomas. Report."

"This is Rigna, Kimar," came the voice. "Hargo and Lomas are with me."

"Good," said Father. "I've got Voldar and Stobo. I'll keep them here in the storeroom of the toy shop. Rigna, you come here and take them off my hands. I want Hargo and Lomas to look for a man named Shim. Tell him to search the caves along the Transfers Canal."

"Can do, Kimar."

Then Father turned to his new prisoners.

"You two—" he said, indicating a storeroom, "in there."

There wasn't much stored in the storeroom, just a few shelves of supplies. "All right, you might as well relax," said Father. "You're going to be here for a while. Sit down."

They did. And Father reached back to shut the

door. With the blaster aimed at them and no other exit available, these villains had no chance of getting away before Rigna arrived.

In the cave, Dropo did his best to stay in the shadows, knowing it was just a matter of time before one of the evildoers realized that he wasn't Santa. When his captor's back was turned, though, he quickly found his way to the control panels. A little movement of a switch, the twisting of a gizmo, the relocation of a red lightbulb and he was ready.

Dropo dashed for the door, pausing when he heard the voice of his captor.

"Where are you going?" asked Shim.

Dropo almost said, "As far away from here as my legs will carry me," but he caught himself and responded with a not terribly-hearty "Ho, ho, ho."

"Can't you say anything else besides ho, ho, ho?"

"Ho, ho, ho," Dropo repeated.

"If you're thinking of leaving, Santa, let me remind you: Once you hit that nuclear curtain, there won't be even a whisker left of you."

"Ho, ho, ho," said Dropo as he dashed past the spot where the invisible curtain once invisibly stood.

"Hey, Santa," called Shim, "be careful."

Shim turned back to the control panel and noticed that the switches were out of place. He corrected them and reactivated the shield, but it was too late.

What would Voldar say? More important, what would Voldar do?

In the storeroom, Voldar, unaware that there were two Santas now on the loose, looked for an opportunity to turn the tables.

"What are you going to do with us?" he asked.

"You're going to stand trial before the council," said Father. "I don't think you'll be causing any more trouble."

Little did Father know that Voldar had been analyzing the items in the room, calculating vectors, weights, and probabilities—and was looking for the best moment to make his move. When he was first locked in here, he had noticed a ski, set across two barrels. How fortuitous that Father would stand near enough to the tip of the ski so that . . .

Voldar struck, forcing his end of the ski down and causing the other to rise rapidly—right into Father's arm. The force knocked the weapon out of Father's hands, suddenly turning this into a fair fight.

Well, almost. Before a fist could fall, Stobo was in the middle of the melee, bouncing back and forth between the two warriors. As he was pushed out of the way, Voldar seized the opportunity to grab a shelf above him and kick Father's feet, in a move reminiscent of the one that would later be popularized by Batgirl on the Earth program *Batman.* Boy, that Batgirl could kick.

So could Voldar, who forced Father back into the wall, where Stobo dealt him a blow to the head with a piece of wood.

Voldar inspected the unconscious man.

One obstacle out of the way.

In the toy workshop, Santa was undoing the damage caused to the manufacturing machine. Midway through the repair, he had considered ripping out some of the wires and declaring the machine inoperative. Then he could train these Martians in the fine art of old elf craftsmanship. The kind of attention to detail you can't get in a store—or from a machine created in a matter of hours by a race of Martian geniuses. "Well, now, I think that ought to do it, Billy boy," said Santa. "Close the door, son."

The mechanical work was done, but Santa, being a perfectionist, needed the machine to look good as well.

"Now, I think we'll need a little red paint," he said. "You'll find it in the storeroom."

"Sure, Santa," said Billy, obediently.

"That's a good boy," said Santa, watching him go.

But something was not right. Santa rubbed his beard and thought deep thoughts.

On his way to the storeroom, Billy heard voices. Yes, they were coming from behind the door. He moved closer to listen.

"This time I'll get rid of Santa for good," he heard, and "smash that machine."

That was enough. Billy sprinted back into the workshop.

"Santa. Santa," said Billy, interrupting Santa's testing of a new kind of varnish made from Mars's Ja'quil bushes. A little sticky. Not very smooth.

"Voldar and another man are in the storeroom and they're coming to get you," insisted the boy.

"Oh, they are, are they?" said Santa. "Eh, well, maybe they'd like to have some fun with our toys.

And we'll see that they do, won't we, kids? Psssst."
And he motioned them in for a huddle, knowing that
they were going to love this idea.

Minutes later, as Santa sat jauntily smoking
his pipe, Voldar burst in brandishing Father's blaster.

"Oh, ho, we meet again, eh," said Santa, playing
the I'm-too-friendly-to-be-scared card.

"I don't know how you escaped Shim," admitted
Voldar, "but you won't escape me. You're through."

"Voldar, why don't you, eh, relax?"

Voldar cocked the weapon.

"You're going to relax," Voldar said, " . . . perma-
nently."

And then the assault began. A children's cru-
sade. First, a steady stream of cold water struck him
in the face. Martians, as you may know, are not big
on water games. The Martianolympid features no
aquatic sports. Bathing is kept to a minimum. In fact,
one of the reasons Martians stayed away from Earth
for so long was because of the massive bodies of
water that dominate your planet. In about eighteen
to twenty years, your scientists will figure out the se-

cret for forcing the ocean below the planet's surface, which opens up a lot of real estate while rendering antique the whole idea of "shoreline."

But you've got a little while until that.

The water was now hitting Voldar from multiple directions. And with Santa laughing hysterically, Billy and Betty and Bomar and I attacked.

With bubbles. And rubber arrows. And bad-minton racquets. And toy cars. And Ping-Pong balls. And balsa airplanes. And toy soldiers. And more bubbles.

Man, how Voldar hated bubbles.

I shot an arrow. A toy Indian drummed. Betty had a bat. I had a toy sword.

LOU HARRY

And Voldar was unable to defend himself.

Something ran over his toe. He hopped like a Crater-roo.

And since Martian children cannot be hurt by Martian adults (not only is that the law, but Chochem figured out a way to make it a part of our antenna programming), there was little he could do.

Just outside the room, Stobo was considering how to switch sides when he backed into . . . another Santa Claus?

"You," said Stobo, confused. "You're not here. You're in there."

"Yeah," said Dropo. "You're right. I'm not here. I'm in there." And he tried to leave, but Stobo grabbed him by the sleeve.

"Wait a minute," said Stobo. "I'm going to see who Voldar's fighting in there."

He peeked through the door. Only to have a red rubber ball shot into his mouth.

"What happened?" asked Dropo.

Stobo spit out the ball. "I don't know what's going on in there. But I'm going to take care of you myself."

He fumbled in his bag for his blaster.

"Now just a minute," said Dropo, trying to stall. "I'd like to talk to . . ."

And the door to the storeroom opened. Father, a little stunned but none the worse for wear, grabbed the weapon from Stobo's grasp. This time, his hands went over his head without having to be ordered.

"Oh boy, Chief," said Dropo, "am I glad to see you."

"There you are, Dropo," said Father. "Inside, Stobo."

The trio entered the workshop. And Father knew with one look that he had never seen a battlefield like this.

"Kids, you can stop now," he said, but the kids were having too good a time.

"I said, 'cease fire!'"

And, as fun as it was, we stopped, knowing that our ruler had spoken and that we were in good hands.

Voldar was in tears. It was kind of pathetic, really.

"All right, Rigna," added Father. "Take them away. They've had a rough day."

Rigna took away Voldar's weapon, and pushed both of the captives toward the door as the kids laughed.

"Ho, ho, ho, everybody," said Dropo, entering the chaos, amazed that there was a major mess that he himself hadn't caused. "Merry Christmas."

Santa smiled at the semi-mirror image of himself and reached out his arms to give Dropo a big hug.

"You don't need me here, Kimar," said Santa. "You've got a wonderful Santa Claus of your own."

Santa was right. We had Dropo Claus.

And Chochem had been right, too. Father had realized that earlier. Chochem hadn't instructed them to kidnap Earth's Santa Claus. The adult Martians had misinterpreted what the wise one had said. Chochem's words were: "We need a Santa Claus on Mars." He never said, "We need *the* Santa Claus on Mars." The Santa we needed was right here all along. Chochem probably realized that, too. On Christmas, Father would make it a point to bring something special to him. But what do you give a guy who can see the future, alter the space/time continuum, and disappear in a puff of smoke? Maybe some deodorant?

LOU HARRY

"Ho, ho, ho," said Santa, and no truer words were ever spoken.

The next day, the children and Santa were ready to leave. Back in their nerdy coats and scarves, they had a tinge of regret at having to leave their host family just as they were beginning to enjoy each other's company.

"Good-bye, Billy. Good-bye, Betty dear," said Mother, tapping foreheads with each. "You take care of yourselves."

"'Bye," said Betty.

"I've got a present for you, Billy," said Bomar, who handed him something. I have no idea what it was. One day, I'll ask.

"Gee, thanks," said Billy.

"Good-bye," said Bomar, remembering the Earth tradition and reaching out his hand to shake.

"Gee, we had fun," said Billy.

"We're sure going to miss you," I told them.

"Do you think we'll ever meet again?" Betty asked.

"I'm sure you will, children," said Mother. "Thank you, Santa, for bringing happiness to the children of Mars."

"And," added Father, "the Christmas spirit to all of us."

"Kimar," said Santa, "from the bottom of my heart, I wish you and yours the very best of everything."

The tender scene was interrupted by the arrival of a suddenly fattened Dropo, wearing the red suit. Never again would we see him without it.

"Ho, ho, ho, Merry Christmas."

"Dropo, you've gained weight," said Mother.

"And no pills. Or pillows. Look," he said, pointing to his stomach.

Father gave Dropo's new belly a tap with his sharp fingernail and we all heard a pop. Dropo was once again as thin as he ever was.

And we all laughed.

Santa bent over to talk to the Earth children. "Now, if we hurry," he said, "we can get back in time for Christmas Eve."

"Yay!" they both cheered.

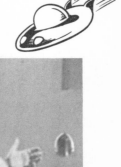

"Shall we get going?" asked Santa.

"Yay!" they cheered again.

"Good-bye, dear friends. Away!!!!"

They turned at the door.

"Merry Christmas, everyone."

And they headed back to Earth in *Spaceship Number 2*, piloted by Rigna. It ran a little slower than *Spaceship Number 1*, but the fact that they had no stowaways in the radar box kept them on schedule.

It would take all the power of our Forget Rays to wipe out this story from the memories of everyone on Earth. In fact, we were just a little bit short. A writer somewhere in the United States failed to get dosed and, apparently, wrote down the story. He managed to get some movie folks to make a low-budget movie based on it. The movie was the subject of much ridicule on Earth. It failed to be nominated for any of their coveted awards of the Academy. Such is the power of Earthling denial.

Still, while we gather each Septober to sing our favorite Martian holiday song, it is comforting to know that some humans just a few million miles away who have seen the film are also singing "Hooray for Santy Claus."

Need a reminder of the lyrics, my Earth friend?

He's fat and round but jumping jiminy
He can climb down any chim-e-ney
When we hear sleigh bells ring
Our hearts go ting-a-ling
'Cos there'll be presents under the tree
Hooray for Santy Claus
Hang up that mistletoe
Soon you'll hear ho, ho, ho
On Christmas day you'll wake up and you'll say
Hooray for Santy Claus

You do remember it, don't you?

Don't you?

Okay, fine. What else?

Is that it?

But there's still some time left on the tape.

Are you sure that's all you need? Do I get one of your Earthling Golden Globe Awards now? I want a Golden Globe Award. I was told I could have one if I told the story to you.

No?

Oh, well, at least you have your Santa Claus back. And Mars has its Dropo Claus. And everyone is happy.

Except for the Venusians. Did you hear what happened with the Venusians? How they came to Mars and tried to kidnap Dropo Claus and . . .

It's the truth. I swear. It happened after I rose to power as Queen of Mars. That was before I came here.

I don't remember how I got here.

I'm kind of tired.

And hungry.

It's been nice talking to you, but I'd like to go back to the dayroom now and get a sandwich. And maybe another snack cake.

'Bye.

LOU HARRY

Addendum

Santa Claus
Conquers the Martians

Trivia

One other thing.

When the Earthlings attempted to make a movie out of the events I've described here, they had to use human actors and Earth locations. This was because of a complicated agreement between the Screen Actors Guild (SAG) and the Federation of Martians Who Pretend to Be Other Martians for the Purposes of Entertainment (FMW-PBOMPE).

Since the movie has developed something of a cult following on Earth, I thought I'd add some facts even its most hard-core fans might not know about its cast and its creation.

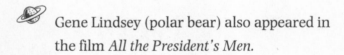 Gene Lindsey (polar bear) also appeared in the film *All the President's Men.*

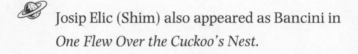 Josip Elic (Shim) also appeared as Bancini in *One Flew Over the Cuckoo's Nest.*

Bill McCutcheon (Dropo) played Leo the Leprechaun on *The Howdy Doody Show,* was a regular on *Sesame Street,* and won a Tony

Award for Best Featured Actor in a Musical (the theatrical equivalent of Best Supporting Actor) for his performance in the 1988 Broadway revival of the musical *Anything Goes.*

 Milton Delugg, who composed the jarring *Santa Claus Conquers the Martians* score, recorded the album *Accordion My Way—Ole!,* served as bandleader on *The Tonight Show,* wrote the theme song for *The Newly-wed Game,* and served as musical director for the Macy's Thanksgiving Day Parade.

 Doris Rich (Mrs. Claus) appeared frequently on the 1950s anthology series *Kraft Television Theatre* and played Ma Kettle in *The Egg and I,* a 1951 series considered television's first comedy serial.

 Director Nicholas Webster went on to helm episodes of *Mannix, The Waltons,* and *Get Smart.* He also wrote and directed the motion picture *Manbeast: Myth or Monster?,* a question we are still asking to this day. By the way, *Manbeast: Myth or Monster?* was a documentary about an Earth creature known as Bigfoot. Let me tell you—because we Martians checked (we don't like to take chances when visiting a planet)—there is no Bigfoot. And there is no Loch Ness monster. And there is no Abominable Snowman. There is, however, a Pete Rose.

Santa Claus Conquers the Martians was, in one video release, retitled *Santa Claus Defeats the Aliens.* In the one you own, it was not.

The film was shot on Long Island. That's a long island near New York City.

The movie was the subject of one of the more popular episodes of *Mystery Science Theatre 3000,* where an Earthling and two robots heckled the entire film? (For example, when the elves are shown, one of these shadowy comics says: "Hmmm, looks like C. Everett Koop's children work here." Just as an aside, I have to wonder what kind of person would spend so much time and energy making fun of an innocent movie? Just asking.)

Vincent Beck (Voldar) played Igor in the episode of *Gilligan's Island* where the castaways are visited by Russian cosmonauts. He also played Ivan the Terrible in an episode of *The Monkees*. Typecasting is hard on an actor. When a movie features an actor cast in the wrong role, you shouldn't be mad and cynical. You should be happy.

 John Call (Santa Claus) appeared on Broadway in *As You Like It*, *Oliver!*, and *A Touch of the Poet*.

The films that bested *Santa Claus Conquers the Martians* at the 1964 Academy Awards (held on April 5, 1965, at the Santa Monica Civic Auditorium) were *Becket*, *Dr. Strangelove or: How I Learned to Stop Worrying and Love the Bomb*, *Mary Poppins*, *My Fair Lady*, and *Zorba the Greek*. While we were rooting for *Dr. Strangelove* (I believe I told you, we like early Kubrick), the ultimate victor was *My Fair Lady*. Best Special Visual Effects went to the crew of *Mary Poppins*. If the Chochem sequence of *Santa Claus Conquers the Martians*

had been animated, it might have had a shot.

🪐 The stock footage of planes refueling was also used in Stanley Kubrick's Cold War classic *Dr. Strangelove*.

🪐 Producer Joseph E. Levine also was executive producer of *The Graduate*, *The Producers*, *Carnal Knowledge*, and *The Lion in Winter*.

🪐 Ned Wertimer (reporter Andy Henderson) played Ralph, the doorman of the building that housed the "de-lux apartment in the sky," on *The Jeffersons*.

🪐 Leila Martin (Lady Momar) originated the role of Madame Giry in Broadway's *The Phantom of the Opera* and stayed with the show for more than 4,500 performances. Can you imagine having to listen to that show more than 4,500 times? Jeez, bring on the Q-ray.

Pia Zadora (Girmar) won a Golden Globe
Award for her performance in the god-awful
movie *Butterfly*, a fact often used to point out
how easy it is for the Golden Globes to be
bought. I'm allowed to be really critical of her
performance, since she played, well, me.

About the Author

Lou Harry has a degree in Film and Media Arts from Temple University. He is also the author or coauthor of *The Encyclopedia of Guilty Pleasures*, *Dirty Words of Wisdom*, *As Seen on TV*, *In the Can: The Greatest Career Missteps, Sophomore Slumps, What-Were-They-Thinking Decisions, and Fire-Your-Agent Moves in the History of the Movies*, and *The High-Impact Infidelity Diet: A Novel*. He first saw *Santa Claus Conquers the Martians* at a very impressionable age.

About the DVD

Santa Claus Conquers the Martians
Directed by Nicholas Webster
Written by Paul L. Jacobson and Glenville Mareth
Produced by Paul L. Jacobson, Arnold Leeds, and
   Joseph E. Levine
Original Music by Milton Delugg
Cinematography by David L. Quaid
Film Editing by William Henry
Art Direction by Maurice Gordon
Set Decoration by John K. Wright III
Costume Design by Ramsey Mostoller
Makeup by George Fiala

Cast

Santa Claus: John Call

Kimar: Leonard Hicks

Voldar: Vincent Beck

Dropo: Bill McCutcheon

Billy: Victor Stiles

Betty: Donna Conforti

Bomar: Chris Month

Girmar: Pia Zadora

Momar: Leila Martin

Hargo: Charles Renn

Rigna: James Cahill

Andy Henderson: Ned Wertimer

Mrs. Claus: Doris Rich

Chochem/Von Green: Carl Don

Winky: Ivor Bodin

Stobo: Al Nesor

Shim: Josip Elic

Lomas: Jim Bishop

Children's TV Announcer: Lin Thurmond

TV News Announcer: Don Blair

Santa's Helpers: Scott Aronesty, Tony Ross,
    Ronnie Rotholz, Glenn Schaffer

Polar Bear: Gene Lindsey